"If I seem arrogant, then I apologize."

Byron laughed softly. "But I'm still of the opinion that farming isn't a woman's job."

"And I'm still equally determined to prove you wrong." Frances stared out at the moonlight on the water.

"You don't have to prove anything to me, Frances. It's yourself you have to convince."

"I know I made the right decision."

"Then my arrogant and conceited opinion shouldn't matter to you," Byron pointed out. He lowered his head as Frances raised hers, and a quivering warmth erupted deep inside her when their lips met.

Frances knew the truth as if she had known all her life. She was in love with Byron, but for her own peace of mind, she must never let him guess it.

YVONNE WHITTAL, a born dreamer, started scribbling stories at an early age but admits she's glad she didn't have to make her living by writing then. "Otherwise," she says, "I would surely have starved!" After her marriage and the birth of three daughters, she began submitting short stories to publishers. Now she derives great satisfaction from writing full-length books. The characters become part of Yvonne's life in the process, so much so that she almost hates coming to the end of each manuscript and having to say farewell to dear and trusted friends.

Books by Yvonne Whittal

Don't miss any of our special offers. Write to us at the following address for information on our newest releases.

Harlequin Reader Service
901 Fuhrmann Blvd., P.O. Box 1397, Buffalo, NY 14240
Canadian address: P.O. Box 603,
Fort Erie, Ont. L2A 5X3

YVONNE WHITTAL

sunset at izilwane

Harlequin Books

TORONTO • NEW YORK • LONDON
AMSTERDAM • PARIS • SYDNEY • HAMBURG
STOCKHOLM • ATHENS • TOKYO • MILAN

For my family,
who have never stopped asking
what happened to Frances,
the ten-year-old girl in
Magic of the Baobab

Harlequin Presents first edition October 1987
ISBN 0-373-11022-7

Original hardcover edition published in 1986
by Mills & Boon Limited

CHAPTER ONE

'WOULD you please repeat that?'

Frances King's incredulous voice echoed through the black and white tiled hall of her parents' home, and she sat down rather abruptly on the chair beside the telephone, her fingers tightening their grip on the receiver until her knuckles whitened.

'What's the matter with you, Frances?' Thomas Atherstone enquired with a hint of impatience in his voice. 'Have you gone deaf, or do we have a bad connection?'

'No, no, it's nothing like that!' Her dark eyes were alight with a joyous excitement which was almost too great to bear. 'I'm having difficulty in believing my good fortune, that's all!'

'Well, you can believe it because it's true,' the lawyer insisted. 'Your offer for the farm, Thorndale, was accepted, and I'd like you to meet me there at ten-thirty this morning so that we can check the stock together before you sign the necessary papers.'

It was true! Her offer for Thorndale had been accepted, but it still sounded too incredibly wonderful to believe and, giving vent to some of her excitement, she exclaimed ecstatically, 'Thomas Atherstone, I love you!'

'Hey, I'm a married man, remember,' he warned laughingly, then he sobered and added sternly, 'ten-thirty, Frances, and don't keep me waiting.'

'I'll be there,' she promised, replacing the receiver on its cradle, and locking her hands together in excitement between her denim-clad knees.

She sat there for several seconds, assimilating the news she had received, and hugging it jealously to herself before she got up and went in search of her stepmother.

She glanced at her wristwatch when she stepped out on to the gauzed-in verandah of the farm house. Ten o'clock. She had plenty of time to get to Thorndale before Thomas Atherstone, she decided, pushing open the screen door and letting it slam shut behind her tall, slender body.

Her dark hair was the colour of a raven's wing in the blazing January sun. It was long, reaching down to below her shoulders, and she had tied it back at the nape of her neck with a pink scarf that matched the pink and white striped blouse she wore with her blue denims.

Olivia King was tending the roses she loved so much when she looked up to see her stepdaughter walking towards her with a lithe, natural grace that accentuated her femininity despite her mode of dress. A wide-brimmed straw hat shaded Olivia's face from the stinging rays of the sun, and her grey eyes smiled at Frances with a warmth and a deep affection which had never faltered during the past thirteen years since her marriage to Frances' father. The birth of a half-brother and sister had in no way altered the relationship between Frances and Olivia. It had, in fact, bonded them all closer together as a family unit, and Frances adored the new additions to the family as much as they adored her.

'I shan't be home for tea this morning, Olivia,' Frances announced while she followed her stepmother's small, still surprisingly slender figure into the shade of the tall jacaranda tree, and she could barely conceal her excitement as she watched Olivia discard her garden gloves and drop them on to the wooden table beside the roses she had picked. 'If Dad wants to know where I am, you may tell him I've gone up to Thorndale.'

Olivia had been taking off her straw hat and was shaking her short auburn curls free when she looked up at her stepdaughter with a start.

'Frances?' she queried, her grey eyes lighting up expectantly, and Frances could no longer conceal the reason for her excitment.

'My offer was accepted,' she explained with an excited laugh, her face radiant with the extent of her happiness.

'Oh, darling, I'm truly delighted for your sake!' Olivia exclaimed as they embraced each other with a mixture of laughter and threatening tears.

'I have to go,' Frances said eventually after a quick glance at her watch. 'Thomas Atherstone instructed me to meet him on the farm at ten-thirty, but I should be home for lunch, and then I'll tell you everything.'

She planted a quick kiss on Olivia's cheek, and she was consumed with such an intense mixture of excitement and impatience that she almost ran to the stone buildings behind the house where her new blue Land Rover was garaged. This was what she had always dreamed about, and her dream had come true at last.

She turned off the road from Mountain View, her father's cattle ranch, and took the road from Louisville leading northwards to Thorndale. The road had been tarred in recent months since the Izilwane Game Park had become a popular tourist attraction, and Frances had no reason to complain about this, since the farm, Thorndale, lay directly alongside the game park.

She put her foot down on the accelerator, and a smile lifted the corners of her mouth as the Land Rover picked up speed. She had worked hard to prove herself capable and to achieve her goal. There had been those years of study at the agricultural college in Natal, and then there had been a further two years of working on someone else's farm for the additional experience before she ventured out on her own. Her mother had died when she was four, leaving her a considerable sum of money which had been wisely invested for her, and which she had inherited when she came of age. Now, at last, she had the opportunity to put that money to good use with the purchase of her very own farm, and the acquisition of a place like Thorndale was a bonus added to the dream she had nurtured for so long.

The Wilkins family had owned Thorndale for more

years than anyone in the Louisville district cared to
remember, and the last owner, George Wilkins, had died
an old bachelor with a reputation for being an eccentric
recluse. It was Frances' father, Bernard King, who had
passed on the information to her that Thorndale had
come on to the market to be sold 'lock, stock and barrel'
to whomever made the best offer for the property and, in
this respect, Frances had not been too proud to rely on
her father's superior knowledge when he advised her as
to what would be considered a reasonable offer for
Thorndale.

This had been a chance in a lifetime. She had always
longed to buy a farm in the Louisville district to be near
her family, but very few farms ever came on the market
and, when they did, they were snapped up almost at
once. Thomas Atherstone had been given the task of
administering the late George Wilkins' estate and, when
Frances had approached him with her offer, he had not
been in a position to give her any firm assurance that her
offer would be accepted. She had to wait a month, like
everyone else, and she had secretly given up hoping when
she received Thomas Atherstone's call that morning.

The entrance to the farm lay directly ahead of her, and
against the fence, on a rusted piece of iron that sagged
sadly to one side, were the barely legible words
'Thorndale—G. Wilkins'. Frances' heart skipped an
excited beat. In her imagination she could see the new
sign she would erect, *Thorndale—F. King*, and the pride
and thrill of ownership quickened the flow of blood
through her veins.

There was a second sign, in a slightly better condition
than the first, attached to the fence. *The Grove—A.
Phillips*. It was a farm that lay beyond Thorndale, but, to
gain access to The Grove, the owner had to pass through
Thorndale property, using the same gravel road Frances
was now driving along to reach Thorndale's homestead.

A. Phillips? Of course, she remembered him now!
Anthony Phillips! They had called him Tony at school.

He was her senior by three years, and Frances could remember vividly that all the girls had been crazy about his fair good looks. She could also recall that he had never been much of a scholar, but the fact that he was a keen sportsman, and captain of the school's rugby team, had enhanced his popularity with the girls, if not always with the teachers.

Frances forgot about Tony Phillips when she saw the sandstone house emerging from among the trees. It was an old but sturdily built house with a shady verandah almost all the way round it, and the colour of the bougainvillaea ranking along the trellised section of the verandah ranged from amber to deep scarlet. The flamboyant trees were flowering, their flame-coloured flowers adding their own splash of brilliance to the deep scarlet poinsettias and the varying colours of the azaleas growing in the surprisingly well-kept garden about the house.

Thomas Atherstone had not arrived yet, and Frances parked her blue Land Rover in the shade of one of the jacaranda trees which lined the avenue leading up to the house. She was glad that she had arrived there before the lawyer since it would give her time to look around on her own, but she was not alone for long.

An elderly black man in khaki shirt and pants was walking towards her, and his leathery face creased into a smile as he removed his wide-brimmed felt hat respectfully. 'Sawubona, Nkosazana.'

'I see you too, Indoda,' Frances returned his greeting in his own language. 'What is your name?'

'Sipho, Nkosazana,' he answered her obligingly.

'You're a Zulu, Sipho. What are you doing here in Venda country?' Frances questioned him curiously.

'My people moved here many years ago with the Wilkins family, and I have been working here on this farm all my life,' he explained, and there was a hint of anxiety in the way he folded and unfolded his hat between his big, calloused hands. 'It is the only home I have ever known, *Nkosazana*.'

'Do you have a wife, Sipho?'

'*Yebo, Nkosazana*. My wife, Gladys, worked in the house for Mr Wilkins, and she is a very good cook.' He studied Frances closely for a moment. 'You are the daughter of *Ufezela*?'

Ufezela—the scorpion. She smiled and looked at him with interest. 'Do you know my father?'

'Everyone knows *Ufezela*,' he smiled broadly, his teeth strong but yellowed. 'He is the big man with the many cattle and the white bird that roars in the sky.'

Her smile deepened with amusement. She had forgotten that the blacks referred to her father's twin-engined Cessna as 'the white bird that roars in the sky'.

Thomas Atherstone's silver-grey Mercedes sped towards the house along the avenue of trees, and pulled up next to Frances' Land Rover. The lawyer was a man in his early forties and balding slightly. His manner was brisk, but friendly, and he took charge at once, unlocking the house with a bunch of keys he took from his jacket pocket and instructing Sipho to arrange with Gladys to have tea waiting for them when they returned to the house.

Frances could feel herself shaking inwardly with excitement when she walked with Thomas Atherstone towards the sorting camps not far from the house into which the Afrikaner cattle had been herded for her inspection.

'There were approximately three hundred head of cattle at the last count, but since then there's been an advent of late calves, and at a rough estimate I'd say the number now adds up to somewhere in the region of three hundred and fifty,' Thomas Atherstone explained.

Frances leaned with her arms on the wooden railings, her eyes narrowed against the glaring sun and the dust as she studied the condition of the agitated, lowing cattle. They were not lean, but she had seen better-looking animals, and she was nodding her approval when the sound of approaching footsteps made her glance over her shoulder to see Sipho walking towards them.

'The cattle are hungry, Sipho,' she addressed the elderly black man. 'You may let them out to feed.'

Sipho did not hesitate. The gates were flung open, and the herd almost trampled each other in their haste to reach the grazing camps while Frances accompanied Thomas Atherstone on a tour of the rest of the buildings.

There were three horses in the stables—two geldings, and one mare in foal. In a shed close by there were a tractor and a jeep with a canvas hood which could be raised when it rained. There was also a large, serviceable truck for transporting cattle. All three vehicles had a slightly battered look about them, but Thomas Atherstone assured Frances that they were still in perfect working order.

A garage, which could accommodate two cars, stood empty, and she glanced about her eagerly while Thomas Atherstone balanced his briefcase on his raised knee to open it and take out several sheets of paper which were stapled together.

'I have here a list of all the tools and implements in the shed and here in the garage. Would you like us to go through it to check the items listed?'

'Good heavens, no!' Frances exclaimed in mock horror, catching a glimpse of a list which seemed interminable. 'I'm most certainly not going to have a fit if a spanner or two happens to be missing.'

'Then I suggest we move on into the house,' the lawyer smiled, with a look of relief flashing across his lean face.

Like most old farmhouses, the rooms were large and cool. There were four bedrooms and a bathroom, and leading off the entrance-hall was a spacious lounge into which George Wilkins had crowded an old but serviceable bench and chairs and a solid oak dining-room table and dresser which could possibly be considered as valuable antiques. The room across the hall might have been used as a dining-room, but it was crammed with stacks of old *Farmer's Weekly* magazines, boxes filled to overflowing with old photographs which could only be of value to his remaining relatives, broken chairs, and various ancient kitchen and household appliances which were no longer of use since the farm had been supplied with electricity some years ago. The curtains in some of the rooms were torn, probably as a result of being washed too often, and in some places the paint had blistered on the walls and had started peeling.

The house had stood locked and with the curtains drawn for six weeks since George Wilkins had passed away, and the furniture was coated with a fine layer of that northern Transvaal dust which somehow manages to seep into a house against all odds, but Gladys, the buxom wife of Sipho, had hastily dusted the dining-room table and chairs before bringing in a tray of tea for Frances and the lawyer.

'*Sanibona*,' she smiled pleasantly, and then she retreated hastily, leaving them alone.

Frances poured, expressing her delight at the delicate china cups. 'George Wilkins may have been a crusty old bachelor with a reputation for being a recluse, but in his eccentricity he obviously had a preference for drinking his tea from expensive china.'

'He was an extremely refined old gentleman in many ways.' Thomas Atherstone looked thoughtful when Frances passed him his cup of tea. 'I never mentioned it, but you might have noticed that beyond the outbuildings there's a fruit orchard that yields at least four types of fruit such as pawpaws, bananas, guavas and oranges. There's a reservoir close to the orchard with an electric pump which supplies the house with water, and the water is also used for the orchard and the garden, but you have nothing to worry about. Sipho, your *Induna*, or Bossboy, can take care of all this for you.'

They drank their tea in silence, then the lawyer lifted his briefcase on to the table, and Frances felt a shiver of excitement race through her when he opened it.

'I have here the necessary documents for your signature. I'd like you to read through them carefully, and if you'd like your father to go through them with you, then you're welcome to take them home with you.'

Frances shook her dark head and smiled. 'That won't be necessary. This is my venture entirely.'

Dammit! Her excitement and happiness were so great that it was an effort to sit still. She felt like rushing outside and climbing on to the roof to whoop so loudly that the whole world could hear her, but instead she had to read through the legal document which the lawyer had drawn up.

'I'm sure you'll find everything in order,' he said, 'but I'd like you to read it all the same so that, if there's anything you don't understand, I can explain it to you.'

She nodded, attempting to look businesslike, and forced herself to read every word typed on the document. It was all quite straightforward; there was nothing that needed explaining, and she had a feeling that she was grinning rather inanely when she looked up to find the lawyer watching her intently.

'What happens when I've signed it?' she asked.

'I shall expect you to bring your bank-guaranteed cheque to my office first thing tomorrow morning,' he smiled at her. 'It will take another two to three weeks before the transfer is through, but, other than that, Thorndale will belong to you.'

'Where do I sign?' she wanted to know with some impatience.

'Right here,' he said, jabbing his bony finger on the dotted line at the bottom of the last page, and offering her his pen. Frances could feel her insides quivering with excitement when she attached her signature to the document and, when she put down the pen, she looked up to see Thomas Atherstone smiling broadly as he held out his hand to her. 'Congratulations, Frances.'

His handclasp was firm, but Frances was so thrilled

she had to suppress the desire to kiss him. 'Is this all there
is to buying Thorndale?'

'Not quite,' he smiled, pushing yet another document
towards her across the table. 'There's a .303 rifle and a
shotgun which are kept in the gun safe, and you have to
sign this paper for their transfer to your name.'

'I hope I shall never have to use them,' she said with
sudden gravity, signing her name where he had
indicated.

Thomas Atherstone left a few minutes later, and this
gave her the opportunity to wander about on her own to
take an unhurried look at the place which was now her
own.

The outbuildings had been built with sandstone
similar to the house, and their corrugated iron roofs were
still in comparatively good condition. The house itself
had a newly-thatched roof which would provide that
much-needed coolness in this bushveld heat of the
northern Transvaal. She was very anxious to see the rest
of the farm, but it would have to wait until she had the
opportunity to bring her own horse up from her father's
farm, Mountain View, and that would not be for a day or
two.

Frances leaned against the wooden railings of the
camp where she had stood earlier that morning with
Thomas Atherstone, and beneath her perfectly arched
brows her dark eyes were staring thoughtfully into the
distance. Her features were strikingly attractive, the kind
that drew appreciative male glances wherever she went,
but she had never had much time for involvements,
casual or otherwise. Her nose was straight and narrow
across the bridge, and her mouth was full, but firmly
chiselled above a chin that was nicely rounded and set
with determination. A flawless skin stretched across her
finely modelled bone structure, and her golden-brown
tan was the result of many hours working rather than
lazing in the sun.

A frown creased her smooth brow. What had, a month

ago, been a slender possibility had now become a reality, and she found herself faced with several pressing decisions which had to be made. Plans were taking shape in her mind, some of which she was convinced her parents would not be too happy with, but they would simply have to get used to the idea that she was twenty-three and old enough to decide her own future.

She loved the smell of the veld and the sound of the birds fluttering and singing in the trees, but it was the call of the hadeda ibis that made her smile and raise her glance to see several of these large birds flying low overhead. Ha-ha-ha-dahah! Ha-ha-ha-dahah! Their raucous call was well-known, but it was rather strange to hear it in the middle of the day when it was more frequently heard at dawn and dusk as they flew to or from roost.

Frances was content to stand there dreaming and making plans, but the sound of a vehicle being driven at speed towards the house made her turn hastily and walk in that direction. It was a Land Rover, but she could see that it was not her father's and, curious about the identity of this unexpected visitor, she walked a little faster to reach the house at about the same time that the Land Rover was brought to a somewhat bucking halt behind her own vehicle.

The man who emerged from the Land Rover was tall, and clad in a short-sleeved khaki bush jacket and khaki pants with sturdy, dusty boots on his feet. His massive shoulders tapered down to lean hips, and the muscles in his arms and thighs seemed to be straining against the confining material stretched over them when he approached her with long strides. The sun was in his dark brown hair, giving it a coppery sheen, and his ruggedly handsome features were deeply tanned. There was a distinct aura about him that gave her the impression he was a man in an authoritative position, and she guessed his age roughly in the region of thirty-six.

'I passed Thomas Atherstone on the main road a few

minutes ago, and he told me that it was *your* offer they accepted for this farm.'

Frances' eyebrows rose in faint surprise. He had made no attempt at a polite greeting. He had simply confronted her with a rather blunt statement in a voice that reminded her of the distant roll of thunder, deep and gravelly, and she glanced beyond him to see *Izilwane Game Park* printed on the door of the ivory-coloured Land Rover he had driven.

'You must be Mr Rockford,' she said, recalling her cousin's enthusiastic description of the man who owned the game park, but Megan O'Brien had omitted to mention his rudeness.

'That's correct,' came the blunt reply.

'I'm Frances King,' she said, extending her hand in an attempt to create a more congenial atmosphere.

'I know.' His tawny gaze held hers, ignoring the hand of friendship she had offered, and, unabashed, she let it fall to her side. If he was attempting to place her at a disadvantage, then he was not going to succeed. 'I would like first option to buy this farm from you,' he said.

Now that *really* shook her, and her eyes widened incredulously. 'But—but I've only just bought the farm, and it's not for sale.'

'But it will be,' he stated arrogantly, his narrowed, tawny gaze sweeping her disdainfully from the top of her dark head down to the elegant boots on her feet. 'I can't see a woman like yourself making a success of farming, and I can almost guarantee that within less than a year you'll be wanting to sell.'

Her back stiffened with indignation. Tall though she was, she had to tilt her head back several centimetres to meet his glance, but she would show him she was not the type that could be easily intimidated. This man had declared war and, if that was what he wanted, then he was going to get it.

'You underestimate me, Mr Rockford.' Her eyes were cold with anger, and so was her voice. 'Thorndale is not for sale, and it never will be, so I suggest you take your offer of a first option to buy, and get off my property.'

His strongly chiselled, sensuous mouth curved in a mocking smile. 'If you change your mind, you'll know where to find me.'

He spun on his heel and walked away from her just as a white Mercedes turned off the road and sped towards the house along the avenue of jacaranda trees. This time her visitor was her father, and Frances was aware that she was shaking with the extent of her anger when her father got out of his car and shook hands with the man from Izilwane. Bernard King was still in remarkably good shape for a man of fifty-one. The greyness in the dark hair against his temples made him look distinguished, and gave one some indication of his age, but his height and physique closely matched that of the younger man's.

They glanced briefly in Frances' direction while they talked, and it was obvious to her that *she* was the topic under discussion, then that obnoxious Rockford man got into his Land Rover and slammed the door shut with unnecessary force. He reversed his vehicle, spun it around, and drove away at a speed that made the dust billow up behind the wheels.

There was a gleam of amusement in Bernard King's dark eyes when he walked towards his daughter. Her anger was obvious to him in the set of her shoulders and the tightness about her nose and mouth that gave her face a pinched look.

'That man is the most conceited——' She broke off with an abrupt exclamation of disgust, at a loss to find the appropriate words with which to express exactly what she thought of the man who owned the game park. 'The ink has barely had time to dry properly on the document I signed this morning, and that—*that man*—comes along asking for the first option to buy the farm from me! But that isn't all! To add insult to injury, he has the *nerve* to tell me to my face that he can't see a woman making a success of farming, and he guarantees—

guarantees, mind you—that I'll be wanting to sell within less than a year!'

She was so angry she was breathing heavily through her flaring nostrils. She could not recall ever being this angry before, and her father's bark of laughter did not make her feel any better. It simply made her anger rise by a few extra degrees until she felt sure that, if she had been a thermometer, she would explode.

'Don't take it so seriously, Frances,' her father warned. 'Byron had pinned his hopes on buying the farm to extend his game park, and try to imagine how you would have felt if you had heard that your offer hadn't been accepted for Thorndale.'

She paused for a moment to consider this, and in the process her anger subsided partially. 'I didn't know he'd also made an offer for the farm, and I guess it's quite understandable that he's disappointed and upset,' she conceded stiffly, 'but I still think he has a nerve!'

Bernard King smiled wryly, and a speculative gleam entered his dark eyes when he studied his daughter. 'I came here for the sole purpose of congratulating you on your success, but instead it appears I've walked into a battle of the sexes!'

'I'm sorry, Dad, but he succeeded in making me so mad that I could——' She gestured expressively with her slender hands, and laughed away her anger. 'Oh, I'm damned if I'm going to let him spoil my happiness and excitement.'

'That's my girl!' her father smiled, opening his arms wide, and she stepped into his embrace to receive his kiss on the cheek and his warm, bearlike hug. 'Congratulations, sweetheart.'

'Thanks, Dad,' she smiled up at him, her encounter with Byron Rockford and her anger forgotten for the moment to be replaced by a glow of excitement as she emerged from her father's embrace, and tugged at his hand. 'Come, let me show you round.'

She knew she was behaving as if her father had never

been to Thorndale before, but he did not mar her enthusiasm by telling her so. He followed her round patiently and tolerantly, listening with interest to the few tentative plans she had made, and offering advice only when it was needed.

Frances glanced at her watch. Twelve-thirty! The past two hours had fled by almost with the speed of lightning, and there was so much she still wanted to show her father.

'I don't suppose there's time for us to saddle up two horses and take a ride out to where the cattle are grazing?' she asked, knowing what the answer would be when she saw her father glance at his watch and raise one heavy eyebrow.

'I'm afraid not,' he shook his head and smiled. 'We're expected home for lunch, and Evalina's getting crotchety in her old age, especially when meals have to be delayed.'

Frances swallowed down her disappointment, and smiled at her father's remark. Evalina was a Venda woman and, ever since Frances could remember, she had been in charge of the kitchen at Mountain View. That was Evalina's domain, and the only other woman who was allowed to intrude was Frances' stepmother. Olivia King had won Evalina's liking and respect with as much ease as she won the liking and respect of everyone who met her, but, as Frances' father had said, she could get crotchety, and especially now in her old age.

'You're right, Dad,' Frances grinned ruefully. 'I want to have a few words with Sipho, the *Induna*, and his wife, Gladys, before I lock up the house, but you go on ahead, and tell Evalina not to wait because I'm on my way.'

'Under the circumstances I'm sure you'll be forgiven for being a few minutes late for lunch, but don't make those few minutes longer than ten,' her father warned when she accompanied him to his car, and Frances did not linger there to watch him drive away.

She turned back and walked at a brisk pace towards

the orchard where she had seen Sipho leading water earlier. Sipho was still there in the orchard, and this time his wife was there with him. Their conversation was grave, and the snatches she had overheard made her realise that they were concerned for themselves. This was exactly what Frances had been afraid of, and it was the reason she had stayed behind to talk to them.

Their conversation ended abruptly when they saw her walking towards them, and they turned to face her proudly. Addressing them with the respect they deserved, Frances took great care in explaining that, although there was a change of ownership, their positions at Thorndale would remain unaltered. She had no intention of making any drastic changes and, until she took charge completely, she was quite happy to leave everything in their capable hands.

Their relieved smiles remained with her during the drive back to Mountain View, but her encounter with Byron Rockford intruded on her thoughts, and aroused her anger once again. Who the devil did he think he was, to come to her with a request for first option to buy Thorndale from her, and how dared he insinuate that she would not make a success of farming?

Frances could understand his disappointment, but his rudeness had been unforgivable. It had also been somewhat startling. Megan O'Brien, her cousin, had not mentioned him often during the three months since Frances' return home, but when she had, it had been with glowing admiration and respect. Megan was not gullible, and her judgement could usually be relied upon, but in this instance she had slipped up badly. Byron Rockford was rude, overbearing, conceited and arrogant, and there were simply not enough adjectives with which to describe what Frances thought of him. The game park bordered on her newly-acquired farm, but she saw no reason for their paths to cross again unless it was absolutely necessary, and she could foresee nothing in the future which would necessitate a second meeting.

The future was, however, unpredictable; Frances could only hope that he would stay out of her way as much as she intended staying out of his.

CHAPTER TWO

LOUISVILLE had not changed very much during the past five years, which Frances had spent mostly in Natal while she had furthered her education. A few new shops now stood in what had once been vacant lots, and a new post office building had been erected in place of the old one, but basically the town had remained the same. The people had also remained unchanged. They were friendly and warm-hearted, like one big family which was never reluctant to take a newcomer into the fold, and Frances smiled at her own thoughts when she crossed the street to where she had parked her Land Rover. She got into it and grimaced. It felt as if she had stepped into an oven, and she hastily turned down all the windows, but there was no breeze to circulate air through the vehicle. This was typical summer weather for the northern Transvaal. It was barely ten o'clock in the morning, and for some the day had scarcely begun, but it was already so hot that the geraniums in the flower boxes ahead of her were wilting in the sun.

Frances turned the key in the ignition, the Land Rover's engine roared beneath her impatient foot on the accelerator, and she pulled away from the kerb, driving through the town and heading out in the direction of Thorndale. She was smiling to herself and humming softly. Nothing, not even the heat of this bushveld country she loved so much, could mar her pleasant mood that morning. Her cheque had been guaranteed by the bank, she had handed it over to Thomas Atherstone to conclude the transaction, and she had made the necessary arrangements at the post office to have the telephone at Thorndale reconnected.

Her smile deepened when she thought about the

family get-together the previous evening. When something momentous occurred, whether it be good or bad, the family always rallied round to offer their congratulations, or their commiserations. The family was small and close-knit, consisting of Vivien and Dr Peter O'Brien, and their daughter, Megan. Vivien O'Brien was Bernard King's only sister, and she was accompanied by Megan when she arrived at Mountain View after dinner the previous evening. Peter O'Brien had not intended to miss out on the family celebration, but at the last minute he had received an emergency call from the local hospital. Frances' father had opened a bottle of champagne to toast her success, and the lighthearted conversation had been conducted amid bursts of excited laughter.

'Are you going to move into the house on Thorndale?' Megan had asked, and the trend of the conversation had changed abruptly from the lighthearted to the grave. 'If you are,' Megan had added, 'may I come and stay with you? It would be so much more convenient for me to get to my shop at Izilwane every day.'

Megan was artistic, sensitive and enterprising. She had opened a curio shop at the game park to sell, among other things, her own work, and the work produced by a local group of Venda artists who specialised in beadwork, pottery and wood-carvings.

Frances had been enthusiastic about the idea of Megan sharing the spacious old house with her at Thorndale, and she had been ready to move in immediately with her cousin, but the family would not hear of it. She was old enough to decide for herself what she wanted to do, Frances had argued the previous evening, but her stepmother and her aunt had insisted that they would like to see the interior of the house on Thorndale before they would agree to Frances and Megan moving in. Frances had relented in the end, and she had left the keys with Olivia early that morning.

Frances' smile deepened with amusement. They were out at Thorndale now, waiting for her, and she wondered what kind of reception she was going to get when she arrived there.

Olivia's new sea-green Jetta was parked in the shade of the jacarandas when Frances arrived at Thorndale. The front door of the house stood wide open, and Frances went inside to find her stepmother and her aunt waiting for her in the lounge-cum-dining-room. Olivia King was smiling at Frances, her grey eyes sparkling with amusement, but Vivien O'Brien's striking features bore the look of someone who could not quite decide whether to laugh or cry.

Frances raised her dark eyebrows with a mixture of mockery and concern as she looked from one to the other. 'Is it *that* bad?'

'No, it isn't,' Olivia answered her calmly, 'but your aunt and I are in agreement. You can't move in immediately.'

'There are several sturdy pieces of furniture which simply need to be cleaned and oiled to accentuate the natural grain of the wood, like this dining-room suite, for instance,' Vivien O'Brien added her candid opinion, 'but the rest of the furniture isn't worth keeping.'

'The interior of the house desperately needs a fresh coat of paint, Frances,' Olivia continued to explain. 'We'll start with the bedrooms, and you can move in when they're ready, but not, I'm afraid, until then.'

'Since Megan is going to be staying here with you,' her aunt chipped in once again, 'Olivia and I have decided to share the expenses between us. We'll put up new curtains, and we'll replace some of the old furniture.'

Frances stared at them incredulously. 'But you don't have to do that!' she protested.

'We want to, Frances,' Olivia said quietly, a tender smile curving her soft, generous mouth. 'Consider it a gift from two people who love you very much and wish you lots of success in your venture.'

A lump rose in Frances' throat, and she tried valiantly

to swallow it down, but the next instant her vision blurred.

'*Dammit!*' She dashed her tears away impatiently with the back of her hand and, laughing self-consciously, she hugged Olivia and her aunt in turn. 'Oh, I love you both so very much, and I don't know how to thank you.'

'We don't need to be thanked, darling,' Olivia smiled, rising to her feet. 'What your aunt and I need at the moment is a cup of tea, and I think Gladys has been waiting for her cue to bring it in.'

Olivia went to the kitchen, leaving Frances alone with her aunt. The family resemblance between the young and the older woman was very strong. Frances' hair was as dark as her aunt's, although Vivien O'Brien's was greying at the temples, but the similarity was undeniable in the shape of the dark brown eyes, the straight nose and the firm mouth. They were also equally tall when they rose at the sound of a car approaching the house.

'It seems as though you have a visitor, Frances,' her aunt announced unnecessarily. 'I'd better warn Olivia that we need an extra cup while you go out and welcome whoever it is.'

Frances obeyed her aunt with obvious reluctance. If it was that despicable Byron Rockford . . . but no! The flashy red BMW parked behind Olivia's Jetta was definitely not Byron Rockford's style, and the man who emerged from it was fair-haired and of an average height. Frances recognised him at once when he came striding towards her. His features were still clean-cut and handsome, and he still walked with that slight swagger she remembered so well.

'Good morning, Miss King,' he smiled, his hazel eyes on a level with her own when he clasped her hand in greeting. 'My name is Tony Phillips.'

'I know,' she returned his friendly smile, removing her hand from his when she felt he had held it longer than necessary. 'We were at school together, but you were a couple of years ahead of me.'

'I was aware of that, but I didn't think you'd remember.' His appreciative glance flicked over her, taking in her slender but shapely body in the pale-lemon, short-sleeved suit she had chosen to wear for her meeting that morning with the bank manager and Thomas Atherstone. 'I hope I haven't arrived at an inconvenient time,' he apologised smoothly, glancing at Olivia's Jetta, 'but I thought I'd drop by and introduce myself since we're going to be neighbours in future.'

'Won't you come in and join us for tea, Mr Phillips?' Frances invited politely.

'Tony,' he corrected, flashing that familiar smile which used to have all the girls at school swooning on their feet, but Frances was still unaffected by it. 'Please call me Tony, and I'll stay for tea, thank you, Frances.'

She took him inside, and the two women seated at the table looked up with curiosity and interest when Frances entered the lounge with her visitor.

'Olivia ... Aunty Viv, I'd like you to meet my neighbour, Tony Phillips,' Frances introduced him. 'Tony, this is my stepmother, and my aunt, Vivien O'Brien.'

'Good morning, ladies,' he smiled, not at all discomfited by their speculative scrutiny. 'Frances very kindly invited me to stay for tea, and it's a pleasure to meet you both.'

Olivia captured Frances' glance when they sat down, and she smiled, giving Frances the impression that she was faintly amused by Tony's gallantry.

'Wasn't George Wilkins your uncle on your mother's side?' Vivien O'Brien questioned him in her charming, unaffected manner while Olivia poured their tea.

'That's correct,' he confirmed, turning to smile into Frances' startled eyes. 'Didn't you know, Frances?

She shook her head. 'I had no idea.'

Olivia passed everyone their tea, and her direct gaze met Tony's. 'If George Wilkins was your uncle, then you must have been a frequent visitor to Thorndale.'

his reasons were for paying her a second visit after their confrontation the day before, but neither had she any desire to find out, and she wished he would leave her alone and go back to Izilwane where he belonged.

'Thanks for the tea, but I'm afraid I can't stay longer,' Byron Rockford announced at last, pushing back his chair and rising to his feet, but his narrowed, tawny glance captured Frances', and held it effortlessly despite her attempts to look away. 'May I have a word with you in private, Miss ... er ... Frances?'

There was a brief, awkward silence while Frances toyed with the desire to send him to the devil, but sheer good manners made her rise from her chair.

'I'll walk with you to your Land Rover,' she said in a cold, clipped voice, and Byron Rockford inclined his head in a curt farewell before he stood aside for her to precede him out of the house.

The smell of the sun and the bush clung to his clothes when she walked with him to where he had parked his Land Rover in the shade of the trees, and it pleased her senses in a way that annoyed her.

'I'd like to apologise for my rudeness yesterday,' he broke the silence between them, and Frances' tight mouth curved in a cynical smile.

'Really?'

'I was serious, however, about buying Thorndale,' he said, ignoring her sarcasm, 'and I have here a written request for first option to buy the farm if you should ever want to sell it.'

She stared at the document he had taken out of the top pocket of his bush jacket, and she felt a wave of anger shuddering through her like a volcano threatening to erupt. 'I have no intention of selling Thorndale.'

'Women are prone to changing their minds, and you might want to change yours in a few months' time.'

Frances tilted her head back, her eyes narrowed against the glare of the sun as she studied his rugged features intently. 'You're convinced that I'm not going to make a success of farming, is that what you're saying?'

'Running a farm is a man's job,' came the blunt, infuriating reply that sent her blood pressure soaring to a new height.

Byron Rockford was not only arrogant and conceited, he was also the most bull-headed man she had ever met, Frances decided in her fury, but his chauvinistic attitude was something she would not tolerate, and she reached out, literally snatching the document from his hand.

'I'll take this written request of yours, Mr Rockford.'

'Byron,' he corrected, his strongly chiselled, sensuous mouth curving in a mocking smile which she would have liked to wipe off his face with the flat of her hand.

'I'll take this written request of yours,' she repeated in a stony voice, 'but, if I'm still here on Thorndale in a year's time, I'm going to make you eat it.'

His mocking smile deepened. 'You're welcome.'

'Goodbye, Mr Rockford!' she spat at him furiously, spinning on her heel and walking away from him with the document he had given her crushed in her tightly clenched hand.

'It's *tot siens*, Frances,' he assured her with a mocking laugh, 'because we'll most certainly meet again, and soon, I hope.'

Not if I can help it! she thought heatedly, her attractive features tight with anger as she looked straight ahead of her, and she was entering the house when she heard him drive away.

Three pairs of eyes looked at her curiously once again when she entered the lounge and rid herself of the offending document by thrusting it into her handbag, but Frances was in no fit state to go into detail about her second confrontation with the man from Izilwane. Byron Rockford might not have intended it so, but his attitude had presented a challenge to her, and she had never been able to resist a challenge. And most especially not when it was directed at her because of her sex.

Tony Phillips announced shortly afterwards that it was

time he left, and Frances walked with him out to where he had parked his car, leaving her stepmother and her aunt to clear away the cups.

'It was nice of you to drop by, Tony,' she thanked him when they reached his red BMW.

'I'll come again, if I may,' he said eagerly, and Frances smiled at the almost boyish look on his handsome face.

'You may not always find me at the house, but you're welcome to come in for a cup of tea when I am,' she assured him.

'My uncle used to let me hunt on Thorndale.' His hazel glance met hers questioningly. 'Would you object if I hunted on your property occasionally?'

'I have no idea what game there is on Thorndale, or in what quantities, but I'm afraid the answer is no, Tony.' Disappointment, and something else which she could not define, flashed across his face, but her decision remained as unfaltering as her gaze. 'I don't agree with the needless killing of game animals, unless their quantity is of such a nature that they're not leaving enough grazing for my cattle, but if there should ever be a need to diminish them in number, then I'll let you know.'

'I'd appreciate that,' he said, his familiar smile flashing once again, then he said goodbye and left.

'We were rather worried about you and Megan living alone here on Thorndale, but it appears you'll have plenty of male company with Tony Phillips and Byron Rockford as neighbours,' her Aunt Vivien announced with a teasing glint in her dark eyes when Frances re-entered the cool, thatched house. 'Tony Phillips has been living alone on The Grove for some years now since the death of his parents, and I imagine it must be lonely for him. Byron Rockford also happens to be a bachelor, but he's not much of a socialiser. The poor man is kept pretty busy, especially during the holiday seasons, but he's a man you could rely on, and I'm glad he's close at hand.'

Frances' expression darkened. Byron Rockford was much *too* close at hand, and she hoped that she would overbearing and pompous, and the less she had to do with him the better.

'What are you going to do now, Frances?' Olivia intruded on her turbulent thoughts, and she frowned down at her elegant suit and white, high-heeled shoes.

'Well, there's not much I can do while I'm dressed like this, so I'm locking up and going back to Mountain View, but as from tomorrow I'm going to be here all day, *every* day,' Frances stated firmly.

The following two weeks were extremely busy for Frances. Her first priority had been to get acquainted with the six herdsmen in her employ and their families, and Sipho, the *Induna*, had assured her of their loyalty. Her black gelding, Pegasus, had been brought to Thorndale from the stables at Mountain View and, with Sipho on one of the other horses in Thorndale's stables, Frances had ridden from camp to camp, inspecting the grazing and the general condition of the Afrikaner cattle. There was not a windmill, or a water trough, that had escaped her notice, and the fences, including the high-security fence between her property and that of the game park, were closely examined.

It was during her first week at Thorndale that Frances had discovered the river camp. It consisted of several acres of good grazing with a section of the river running through it, and it jutted rather deeply into the grounds of the game park. She gave the latter no thought at all; it was that section of the river which appealed to her, and made her realise that she had actually found what she had been looking for. It was a clear piece of land without trees on the rise of the hill on the north-eastern boundary, and it was ideal for the herd of twenty white stud Brahman cattle which she had recently acquired. There were nineteen heifers, most of them in calf, and one young bull. Her father had agreed that she could keep the herd temporarily at Mountain View, but, after inspecting the river camp, she had had the herd brought to Thorndale in her father's trucks.

During those first two weeks, while Frances had been busy elsewhere on the farm, her stepmother and her aunt had taken charge of the house. A painter, and his crew of two from Louisville, had been assigned the task of scraping down the interior walls and giving them a fresh coat of paint, while Olivia and Aunt Vivien took care of the rest. It had been decided that the room across the hall from the lounge was to be used as a dining-room, but Frances had insisted that it should remain untouched until after she had moved in. Among all the rubble and piles of magazines she had noticed an ancient teak desk, and the possibility that it might contain old documents about the farm was something she wanted to investigate for herself before the room was cleared for the painters.

Frances and her cousin, Megan O'Brien, moved into the house in a flurry of excitement on the Saturday morning, a little more than two weeks after Frances had bought the farm. Frances arrived in her loaded Land Rover with Major, a five-month-old golden-haired Rhodesian ridgeback which had been a gift from Logan and Janet, her half-brother and sister, and Megan arrived some minutes later in her equally loaded white Mazda with Pickles, her Maltese poodle. The two dogs sniffed at each other warily, decided they liked each other, and raced off through the garden.

'Something tells me they'll make a formidable team when it comes to protecting us,' laughed Megan, her blue eyes dancing. 'If they're not too busy playing, that is.'

'Oh, yes,' Frances added with mock gravity. 'Major will go for the throat to kill, while Pickles will go for the heels to maim.'

Neither of them could see their animals doing anything of the kind, and they giggled as they entered the house, leaving Sipho and Gladys to off-load their vehicles.

Frances was astounded at what her stepmother and

her aunt had achieved during the past two weeks, and Megan was equally impressed. The fresh coat of white paint on the walls had lightened the rooms, and everything looked so gay and feminine in plain pastels and bright florals. Beds with padded headboards replaced the old-fashioned beds in some of the bedrooms, new carpets partially covered the wooden floors which were now gleaming with polish, and the old wooden bench and chairs in the lounge had been replaced by two comfortably padded sofas and four armchairs in beige and olive-green stripes to match the curtains at the window.

On the dining-room table, which had been cleaned and oiled to bring out the beautiful grain of the wood, stood a vase of roses which could only have come from Olivia's rose garden at Mountain View, and there was a note propped up against it.

Welcome to your new home, Olivia had written in her neat handwriting. *Your aunt and I hope you like what we've done, and we wish you all the happiness and success you wish yourself. Olivia.*

It was a gesture so typical of Olivia. It was so touching, and so heart-warming, that Frances wanted to cry, but she hastily blinked away her tears before Megan noticed.

Megan was three years younger than Frances. She was small and slender with honey-gold curls framing her delicate features, and for some peculiar reason Frances had always felt protective towards her cousin, but Megan did not need to be protected. She was strong beneath that deceptively frail exterior, and her gentle, warm-hearted nature made her easy to befriend.

The two girls spent the day unpacking, and adding their own personal touch to the house with the mementos and the books they loved, while Gladys plied them with numerous cups of tea and a light salad lunch. Frances was impatient to get into the front room, and she was carrying out a pile of dusty magazines which could be thrown away when she heard a vehicle drive up to the house.

'See who that is, will you, Megan?'

'Oh, I forgot to tell you,' said Megan, following Frances into the kitchen. 'Byron has been wanting to see you all week, but he's been busy, and so have you, so he said to tell you he would be coming over this afternoon to speak to you.'

'Well, I don't want to speak to him!' Frances' face was set in a rigid mask as she walked on through the kitchen and out on to the back verandah with Megan in tow.

'Why not?' asked Megan innocently. 'Why don't you want to speak to Byron?'

'Mr Rockford and I have nothing at all to say to each other,' insisted Frances, her expression darkening with obvious dislike.

'If you'd only give yourself the opportunity to get to know him, then I'm sure you'd like him, Frances.'

'I don't *want* to get to know him, thank you very much!'

'Frances!' Megan stared up at her cousin, her blue eyes wide and incredulous. 'This doesn't sound like you at all!'

'Anyone at home?' a now familiar deep voice demanded from the direction of the hall.

'We're coming, Byron!' trilled Megan, then she cast a quick, anxious glance at her cousin. 'Get rid of those filthy magazines, Frances, and for goodness' sake come and be nice to the man.'

Megan turned on her heel with a swish of her floral cotton skirt, leaving Frances alone out on the back verandah. Sue dumped the pile of magazines on to the concrete floor with a force that sent a cloud of dust rising into the air.

Damn the man! she thought, frowning down at her dusty hands and her equally dusty and faded blue denims. What does he want this time?

Gladys was switching on the electric kettle and setting

out a tray when Frances entered the kitchen. 'I'll make tea and bring it to the lounge, missy.'

'Thank you, Gladys,' Frances smiled into that friendly face, but her expression was stony once again when she walked down the passage to the bathroom to wash her hands.

Her face was devoid of make-up, and her long hair was tied back in the nape of her neck with an elastic band, but that did not bother her at all. She had never laboured under the desire to impress anyone with her appearance, and she would not start now with Byron Rockford.

He rose politely from the depths of one of their chairs when she entered the lounge, his tawny gaze giving her no indication as to his thoughts when it flicked over her. 'Good afternoon, Frances.'

'Good afternoon,' she responded stiffly, seating herself in the chair furthest away from him, and wondering if he ever wore anything other than khaki pants and bush jacket.

'Will you have tea with us, Byron?' asked Megan when he had seated himself again with his long, muscular legs stretched out in front of him.

'Thank you, I would like that,' he smiled, his rugged features softening miraculously when his glance rested on the younger girl, and Frances felt her heart do an odd flip-flop.

'I'll go and ask Gladys to——'

'Gladys knows,' Frances interrupted her cousin before she could rise from her chair and leave Frances alone with Byron. 'She told me she'd make tea and bring it to the lounge.'

'Oh,' said Megan, grasping, but not understanding, Frances' behaviour, and an awkward little silence followed.

'I must say the place has changed considerably since the last time I was here.' Byron cast a sweeping glance about the room before his eyes met Frances'. 'It's very nice. Very . . . feminine,' he added as if to stress the fact that he considered a woman's place was in the home and not at the reins of a farm, and she felt herself stiffen with anger.

'Yes, isn't it?' her abrupt, sarcastic response drew a pained look from Megan, and a derisively mocking smile from Byron before he diverted his attention to the fair-haired girl.

'What are you going to do about a studio here on the farm, Megan?' he questioned her.

'I can paint and sketch anywhere,' Megan explained, 'but I have my studio at my parents' home in town, and I shall, of course, be spending my weekends there.'

'That means you'll be alone on the farm at the weekends, Frances,' he remarked conversationally.

'Not necessarily,' Frances responded without explaining the possibility that her young brother and sister might occasionally spend a weekend with her at Thorndale, and he did not pursue the subject as Gladys entered the room with a tray of tea.

'*Sawubona, Mnumzane*,' Gladys greeted Byron respectfully when she had placed the tray on the low table close to Frances.

'*Yebo, Sawubona*,' Byron returned the greeting in her own language, and she flashed a toothy smile as she turned to leave, the floorboards shuddering beneath her weight with every step she took.

Frances poured the tea and, while they drank it, she listened with interest to their conversation, but she did not participate in it. Their discussion involved an advertising company in Johannesburg for whom Megan had done some work in the past to help promote the game park. Because of the quality of work she had produced, she had been approached by a publishing company to illustrate one of their authors' books, and it was a project for which Byron appeared to share Megan's excitement and enthusiasm.

'Is there perhaps anything I could do while I'm here to help you get settled in?' offered Byron.

'Well...' Megan began, and Frances knew she was thinking about the heavy teak desk which they wanted to move to the small room down the passage from the kitchen, but she was not going to let anyone touch that desk until she had gone through its drawers, least of all Byron Rockford.

'Thank you, but we'll manage,' she intervened abruptly, and Byron lifted his massive shoulders in a careless gesture.

'I'll take this tray through to the kitchen, and I still have a few things to do in my room.' Megan prepared to make an exit.

'There's no need for you to leave, Megan,' insisted Frances, reluctant to be left alone with the man whose tawny gaze was beginning to unnerve her.

'I think Byron would prefer to talk to you privately,' Megan persisted, rising determinedly and picking up the tray. 'I'll see you on Monday, Byron.'

Megan walked out of the lounge, leaving Frances alone with Byron, and Frances felt her insides coil themselves into an unfamiliar knot. She was not nervous, she told herself. She was simply preparing herself for the third round in a battle which she began to suspect would never end, and when she looked into those tawny eyes regarding her so intently she had a strong suspicion that she knew what the topic of conversation was going to be.

Thorndale. He wanted her farm, and it seemed as if he was going to pester her relentlessly in his determination to get it.

CHAPTER THREE

FRANCES had an extraordinary feeling that she and Byron were circling each other mentally like animals in an arena, trying to decide when and how to strike. The tension in the lounge at Thorndale was reaching an unbearable level, and it was Frances who decided to make the first move.

'I understood from Megan that you've been wanting to speak to me about something this past week.'

'Yes, there's a certain matter of importance I've been wanting to discuss with you,' said Byron, leaning back in the chair and lacing his fingers together across his broad chest. 'You happen to have a piece of land that juts quite deep into the game park.'

She was beginning to suspect the reason for this discussion, and she could feel the leash on her temper becoming frayed. 'You're talking about the river camp, I presume?'

'That's correct,' he nodded curtly. 'I'd like to buy that piece of land from you.'

Frances had seldom been so close to losing her temper with anyone, and she might have said regrettable things if her dog, Major, had not created a diversion at that precise moment by bounding into the house with Pickles, Megan's poodle, scampering hard on his heels. Pickles took one haughty look round the room before going in search of Megan, but Major, the traitor, had the nerve to approach Byron to have his ears fondled before he collapsed, panting, at Frances' feet.

This incident had taken no more than a minute, but it had given Frances sufficient time to control herself before she replied to Byron's request in a voice that was deceptively calm. 'The river camp is ideal for my herd of

Brahman stud cattle, and it's the only part of the farm that has a section of the river running through it.'

'You have plenty of good grazing ground elsewhere for your Brahman, and you don't need the river water, so you might as well sell the river camp to me now, because in less than a year I shall be buying the entire farm from you,' he argued with an arrogance that was making it increasingly difficult for her to cling to her self-control.

'The river camp is not for sale and, if I were you, I wouldn't be too hasty in planning the extension of your game park on to Thorndale property,' she said icily. 'I may be a woman, Mr Rockford, but there's nothing you could teach me about being a cattle rancher that I don't already know. I can't predict the future, but I'll fight whatever comes between me and success, and . . . I don't give up easily.'

A cynical smile curved his sensuous mouth. 'Determination is a good thing, but stubbornness could lead to your downfall.'

Frances rose to her feet in one lithe, graceful movement to stand tall and proud and outwardly calm, except for the leaping flames in her dark eyes and that angry pulse beating rapidly at the base of her throat.

'Was there anything else?' she asked coldly as Byron calmly followed her example and got to his feet, his height alone making her feel as if she had shrunk in size.

'I've said everything I came to say, and I suggest you think it over carefully,' he persisted.

'I don't have to think it over, and as far as I'm concerned, Mr Rockford, you've outstayed your welcome,' she stated her feelings quite bluntly. She was rewarded with a flicker of anger in his tawny eyes while he observed her from his great height, but it was gone the next instant.

'I think I like you, Frances.' His rugged features creased into a mocking smile. 'You've got plenty of spunk, and I like my women that way.'

'I shall never be one of *your* women, Mr Rockford,' Frances protested distastefully.

'Is that a challenge?' he demanded softly.

'No!' she snapped furiously. 'It's a statement of fact.'

'Too bad!' he shrugged, and Frances felt an embarrassing warmth surge into her cheeks when his assessing, faintly insolent gaze trailed down the length of her body and up again to linger briefly on her small breasts thrusting against the cotton of her pink shirt. She could feel her body reacting in the strangest way to this man's appraisal, and the breath seemed to leave her lungs when his glance shifted higher to rest on that angry pulse at the base of her throat. 'You'll never know what you've missed,' he added with a suggestive, sensual twist of his chiselled mouth.

Frances felt as if she was floundering in deep, unfamiliar waters, and Byron was gone before she could think of a suitable reply. She was shaking with fury as she stood there in the shaft of afternoon sunlight coming through the lounge window, but it was not fury that was making her nerve ends quiver with a new awareness which she was suddenly too frightened to analyse.

Damn the man! *Damn him!*

She stormed out of the lounge and into the room across the hall with her dog at her heels, but Major left the room hastily when she started slamming things about needlessly to give vent to her anger. Megan joined her there a few minutes later, and she studied Frances with wide, curious blue eyes.

'That was a very quick discussion,' she remarked casually.

'There wasn't much to say,' Frances informed her cousin while she slammed one pile of magazines on top of another with a force that made the dust fly. 'He wanted to buy the river camp because it happens to jut into his game park, and I told him it's not for sale.'

'Oh?'

'As a matter of fact,' Frances continued furiously, 'he

has visions of buying the entire farm since he's of the opinion that, being a woman, I'm bound to be a failure.'

'Oh, Frances!' Megan exclaimed laughingly. 'You shouldn't let it upset you so much.'

'Oh, shouldn't I?' Frances demanded, her voice sharp and brittle with sarcasm and anger.

'Men are all the same, and Byron is merely acting true to form,' Megan reasoned with her. 'They think of women as fragile, helpless creatures with little or no sense, and it's up to us to make them see how wrong they are.'

Frances felt some of the tension ease out of her shoulders. This was not the first time she had been discriminated against by some chauvinistic male, and in the past she had fought and won her battles without losing her temper. Why was she allowing Byron Rockford to succeed where others had failed?

'Let's saddle up and go for a ride,' she suggested when she couldn't find an answer to her query. 'We can go on clearing this room when we get back.'

Megan did not object to Frances' suggestion. She changed quickly into a pair of old denims and riding boots, and half an hour later they were racing across the open veld with Frances on Pegasus and Megan on Juniper, the dapple-grey gelding from Thorndale's stables. Pegasus was a spirited horse, but Frances was a spirited rider who had almost been born into the saddle, while Megan had learnt to ride much later in her life. It was, in fact, Frances who had taught Megan to ride when they were children, but Megan had always remained rather wary of horses, and Juniper, tame and reasonably placid, suited her needs perfectly.

Frances felt her tension and anger ease out of her body during the ride. The smell of horseflesh and leather, and the sheer enjoyment of riding, had always had that soothing effect on her. She glanced at Megan and saw her cousin smiling, conveying her own enjoyment as Frances took her on a brief tour of a section of the farm.

'I'd still like to do a painting of you on your horse,' said Megan, her voice raised above the sound of thundering hooves.

Frances smiled at her without answering. Megan had been wanting to do a sketch or a painting of her for some time, but Frances was by nature much too restless to sit still for longer than a minute and, as a result, Megan had several unfinished sketches which she had been forced to relinquish in the initial stages.

The sun was starting its fiery descent and the shadows were lengthening when they left the horses at the stables and walked back to the house. Frances felt refreshed, Megan's cheeks were flushed, and they had both worked up a ravenous appetite.

Gladys had cooked them an enormous meal for that evening. There was succulent steak with fresh vegetables from the garden Sipho tended so lovingly in his spare time, and Frances and Megan attacked their plates at the dinner table as if they had not eaten for several days. After dinner they drank their coffee out on the cool, darkened verandah, where they could listen to the night sounds and watch the moon rising in the star-studded sky, but Frances soon became restless. They took their empty cups to the kitchen, and resumed their task of clearing out the only room in the house which still needed a coat of paint on its walls before the new curtains were hung at the window.

Frances was sorting through the papers and books in the desk drawers while Megan was dumping unwanted objects into cardboard boxes, and piling everything into a corner to be removed and discarded in the morning. Frances worked systematically, casting aside papers and books which were of no importance to her, and clipping together those which she wanted to study at her leisure. She was leaning across the desk, shifting a pile of papers to make room for more, when she noticed an object which had been thrust between the desk and the wall in the corner of the room, and she removed it carefully to find herself staring at a dust-covered but lifelike portrait of the late George Wilkins.

She lifted the portrait on to the desk and propped it up against the wall. 'Well, good evening, Mr Wilkins,' she murmured absently, smiling as she stood back to examine it.

'*What?*' shrieked Megan, her face white and her hand clutching at her throat in terror, but she sagged against the wall with a self-conscious laugh when she saw the portrait. 'For one terrible moment I thought you'd seen his ghost,' she explained weakly.

'This is George Wilkins, previous owner of Thorndale, and Tony's uncle,' Frances introduced Megan to the man in the portrait.

'Tony?' Megan queried confusedly.

'Anthony Phillips, my neighbour who lives on The Grove,' Frances enlightened her cousin.

'Oh, *him*!' Megan's brow cleared and she rolled her eyes in a mock swoon towards the ceiling. 'He's *terribly* good-looking.'

'Uh-huh,' Frances agreed absently, her thoughtful glance resting on the portrait with its broad and unusual metal frame. 'I wonder why the eccentric old man hid his portrait away in the corner behind the desk.'

'He probably didn't like the look of himself. Few people do, but I think Tony's uncle George looks quite a sweet old man,' was Megan's opinion when she crossed the room to study the portrait Frances was dusting down.

'It's dated four years ago, so it's quite a recent portrait.'

'An odd frame, though,' murmured Megan, tapping the frame with her finger. 'It's some sort of light-weight metal which has been sprayed with gold to give it a bronzed effect, I would say, and I find that odd since they are making such beautiful wooden frames these days.'

'Hm . . . it does look odd,' Frances agreed thoughtfully, a little shiver racing along her spine when she fingered the frame, and she looked up to see Megan glancing at her curiously.

'What are you going to do with the portrait?'

'Tony might want it,' Frances decided. Tony was, after all, a nephew of George Wilkins, and the portrait ought to mean more to him than anyone else. 'I'll ask him when I see him again.'

'I've got a feeling that Tony's uncle George is laughing at us behind his white whiskers.'

Frances glanced sharply at her cousin, and laughed. 'Come on, let's have a bath and go to bed. We're tired, and beginning to imagine things.'

Tony Phillips put in an appearance at Thorndale shortly before noon on Sunday morning, looking debonair and handsome in grey slacks and a blue, open-necked shirt. Megan was delighted to meet him simply because he was extremely good-looking, but Frances was glad to see him for a totally different reason. He had arrived at a time when his male strength was most needed. Frances had cleared the front room with the help of Megan and Gladys, and the teak desk, its wood cleaned and oiled, needed to be shifted. Sipho was there to help, and he and Tony laboured under the weight of the heavy desk as they carried it from the front room, across the hall, and down the passage to the small room which Frances was planning to convert into a study.

'Thanks for your help, Tony,' Frances smiled at him when the desk had been positioned to her satisfaction. 'Would you like to stay and have lunch with us?'

'I was hoping you'd invite me,' he grinned back at her, mopping at the beads of perspiration on his forehead with his white handkerchief, and Frances felt a twinge of sympathy for him when she thought of him living alone on The Grove.

They had lunch at the dining-room table in the lounge, and Gladys had cooked yet another enormous meal which left them feeling lethargic and reluctant to move.

'I've got something to show you,' Frances told Tony when they had had their tea and, with Megan accompa-

nying them, they went into the room across the hall.
'There are two boxes of old family photographs.'

Tony glanced frowningly in the direction Frances was
pointing, and he shrugged carelessly. 'Get rid of them.'

'Is there no one else in the family who might be
interested enough to want them?' Frances persisted.

'The only family I know about is a cousin, Claudia de
Leur,' he enlightened her, frowning slightly. 'Claudia's
mother and my mother were Uncle George's only sisters,
but I have no idea where Claudia is living at the moment,
and I don't somehow imagine that she would be
interested in a box of old photographs.'

'We also found this,' said Frances, propping the
portrait of George Wilkins against the wall, and stepping
out of the way for Tony to look at it.

'Good lord!' he exclaimed in surprise, studying the
portrait. 'The miserable and mean old man himself!'

'Oh, we don't think he's miserable and mean, do we,
Frances?' Megan intervened defensively. 'We think he's
rather nice.'

'You didn't know him as well as I did,' Tony smiled
wryly.

'Since you're the closest of his two remaining relatives,
Tony, perhaps you might like to have this portrait of your
uncle?' Frances suggested.

'No, thank you,' he laughed, waving away her
suggestion with an expressive gesture as if he found his
uncle's portrait repulsive. 'You may get rid of the portrait
along with the rest of the photographs.'

'Oh, we can't do that!' protested Megan, her blue eyes
wide and vaguely shocked.

'Why not?' Tony demanded, glancing at her.

'I don't know,' she began hesitantly, glancing at the
portrait of George Wilkins with his white hair and
whiskers. 'It somehow seems such a shame, and it would
feel as if we were evicting an old man from the only home
he ever knew and cared about.'

A profound silence followed Megan's explanation, and

Frances had to admit that she agreed with her cousin. The portrait might not appeal to Tony, but they could not simply cast it aside and destroy it as if it were nothing at all.

'Well, I'll leave the two of you to decide what you want to do with it, but I definitely don't want it,' Tony insisted adamantly. 'Not even if it was framed in solid gold,' he added with a twisted smile.

Frances found his attitude strange, but then, she supposed, tastes differed as much as opinions, and it was possible that Tony's uncaring attitude merely hid his sorrow at having lost the uncle who had been so close to him.

Tony stayed until after tea that afternoon, and they were walking with him to where he had parked his red BMW when Megan announced jokingly, 'If every weekend is like the one we've just had, then you're certainly not going to be lonely, Frances.'

'You've had a stream of visitors since you moved in?' Tony asked with interest.

'Byron was here yesterday afternoon, and today we've had the pleasure of your company,' Megan explained before Frances could answer him.

'I see.' Tony looked thoughtful. 'Has Rockford become a regular visitor to Thorndale?'

For one fleeting moment Frances suspected that he might be jealous, but she cast the thought aside as ridiculous.

'I wouldn't say he has become a regular visitor,' she answered Tony's query gravely, hiding her displeasure at the memory of Byron Rockford's visits behind a shuttered expression. 'He's been here three times, to be exact.'

'On business, or pleasure?'

'Business,' Frances answered with a tight smile.

'Pleasure,' Megan announced simultaneously, contradicting Frances' statement, and a blush of embarrassment stained her cheeks beneath Frances' sharp glance.

'Well, perhaps it was a bit of both,' Megan added lamely.

'I'm afraid I have to go, ladies,' Tony smiled, but Frances noticed that the smile did not quite reach his eyes. 'Thanks for the lunch, and I'll see you around, Frances.'

Megan sighed heavily when he drove away. 'He's nice, and I think he's got an eye on you, Frances.'

'Don't be silly, Megan!' Frances protested crossly. 'Tony and I barely know each other.'

'So what!' shrugged Megan, glancing slyly at Frances as they entered the house. 'I think he's got competition, though.'

Frances' dark gaze was threatening. 'If you're referring to Byron Rockford, then you're——'

'I never said a word,' Megan interrupted, her smile teasing and her hands raised in a gesture of surrender.

Frances tried to laugh off their conversation, but inwardly she felt uneasy and agitated. The very last thing she wanted at that moment was an emotional involvement with a man. She was beginning to like Tony. He was easy-going and pleasant company, but that was all she ever wanted it to be. Byron Rockford? Well, that was a different matter entirely. She disliked the man intensely, and there was no possibility of any kind of relationship between them, friendly or otherwise.

'What are you going to do with Uncle George?' Megan asked that evening after they had had something to eat and were drinking their coffee out on the darkened verandah. Frances had been so deep in thought that it took several seconds for her to realise that Megan was talking about the portrait.

'I don't know,' Frances murmured thoughtfully. 'What do you suggest?'

'I think Uncle George's portrait would look very nice in the lounge,' Megan offered her opinion, then she giggled unexpectedly. 'That way he can keep his approving, or disapproving, eye on us, don't you think?'

'I think I like that idea,' Frances confessed. She could

imagine *Uncle George* raising his bushy eyebrows at the modern farming methods she intended to implement.

'Did you also get the feeling that Tony didn't like his uncle very much?' Megan asked unexpectedly.

'I can't say that I did,' Frances shook her head and stretched lazily, and her chair creaked, mingling with the sound of the crickets in the undergrowth. 'Perhaps they simply didn't see eye to eye about certain things, but I wouldn't say he disliked his uncle.'

The conversation ended there, but Frances found that she was thinking about the things they had discussed when she went to bed that evening. Megan was usually very perceptive, that was one of the reasons why she was such a good artist, but she must be mistaken about Tony. Would he have taken the trouble to help his uncle get his supplies from town if he had disliked him?

No, of course not! Megan must be wrong, Frances decided, plumping up her pillows and going to sleep almost the minute she put her head down.

Frances was on Pegasus two days later, inspecting the herd of Afrikaner cattle in one of the camps, when Sipho came racing towards her on horseback in the shimmering midday heat as if the devil himself was chasing him.

'*Nkosazana!*' he said breathlessly when he reined in beside her. '*Ucingo lunqanyuliwe!*'

'The fence has been cut?' Frances repeated incredulously, her heart thudding anxiously in her breast. 'Where, Sipho?'

'The river camp, *Nkosazana*,' he informed her, his eyes wide in his black, weatherbeaten face. 'The impala are walking with the cattle, and there are three Brahman missing.'

Frances was so shattered that she could not think straight for a moment. Never, not even in her wildest dreams, had she imagined she would ever encounter a situation such as this, for no one in their right mind would dare to cut the fences which had been erected between farms, and most especially not between a farm and a game park. Who on earth would do such a damnable thing?

'Get a few of the herdsmen together at the river camp, and see what you can do, Sipho, while I go home and try to get in touch with the *Umlungu Omkhulu* at Izilwane,' she rapped out the instruction to her *Induna*, her hands tightening convulsively on the reins at the prospect of having to confront Byron Rockford.

'*Yebo, Nkosazana*,' Sipho agreed at once, and they swung their horses round, racing in opposite directions.

Umlungu Omkhulu—the big white man. That was what Sipho called Byron Rockford, and Frances had adopted the use of that name quite naturally. She had to let him know that the fence had been cut between her farm and his game park, but she did not even want to begin to think what the *Umlungu Omkhulu* would say when she told him that some of his impala had escaped on to her property while three of her Brahman cattle had wandered into his.

Frances leaned forward in the saddle, the wind whipping into her face and lifting her makeshift ponytail from her shoulders. She had to hurry. She had no idea when and how that fence had been cut, but now there was no time to lose. She had to get in touch with Byron Rockford and, much as she disliked the idea, she had to turn to him for assistance.

She did not have to use the telephone to contact Byron at Izilwane. She was still tethering Pegasus to the verandah rails when the Land Rover from the game park sped towards the house, stopping a few metres away from her in a cloud of dust. Byron Rockford emerged from the vehicle and, slamming the door, he came striding towards her on those long, muscular legs with a ferocious expression on his ruggedly handsome face.

'What the devil did you think you were doing when you cut the fence between the river camp and my property?' he demanded in a thundering voice when he stood towering over her with his hands resting on his lean hips.

'Now wait a minute!' she began, too stunned and incredulous to be angered immediately by his surprise attack. 'Are you accusing *me* of cutting the fence?'

'Who else would have adequate reason to do something like that?' he snarled down at her derisively. 'I'm well aware of the fact that the game on your farm has almost been depleted by that young fool from The Grove, and what better way to increase your stock than by cutting the fence to lure them on to your land so that you may hunt the animals down whenever the whim takes you?'

Now that really angered her. She could accept his rash accusation that she had cut the fence; she might have made the same spur-of-the-moment accusation had she been in his position, but she would not tolerate his blatant and uncalled-for attack on her character.

'I'm not in the habit of hunting down animals for the fun of it, Mr Rockford, and if you knew me better you would know that,' she stormed at him, her hands clenched at her sides, and her dark eyes blazing up into his. 'And since you're flinging around accusations, I might as well take this opportunity to get in one of my own. How do I know you didn't cut the fence to spite me, or in the hope that this incident might pressurise me into selling the river camp to you?'

His head jerked back as if she had struck him, the sun setting fire to his deceptively dark-brown hair, and his mouth tightened with displeasure in his grim face. 'I offered to buy the river camp, you refused to sell, and that was *that* as far as I was concerned.'

'So that leaves me as the guilty party, does it?' she bit out the words, and she could feel herself start to shake with fury. 'Well, I don't *want* your impala on my land, Mr Rockford, so I suggest you get them off as soon as possible and back on to your property where they belong. All I happen to be interested in are my three Brahman heifers that strayed on to your land. At this precise moment I can't afford a loss like that, and I want them back.'

'My game wardens have found your blasted cattle! That's how I discovered that the fence was cut, and my wardens are, at this very moment, relinquishing their more important duties to herd your cattle back into your river camp,' he informed her with a savage anger darting from his tawny eyes. 'If I were you I'd think carefully before you cut the fence a second time, and, if I'm to believe that *you* didn't do it, then I suggest you find out who did.'

'None of the workers on my farm would ever do anything as despicable as cutting a fence,' she replied acidly. 'Can you guarantee that of *your* employees?'

'I most certainly can!' came the savage answer to her query. 'Good day, Miss King!'

'Just a minute!' she stopped him when he was striding away from her to where he had parked his Land Rover. 'What about the impala that got through on to my land?'

He turned, looked her up and down in her white shirt, dusty denims and equally dusty riding boots, and a look of disdain flashed across his rugged, deeply tanned face. 'Consider them a gift!' he gestured angrily with his hand.

'I don't want——' Frances began indignantly, but he had got into his Land Rover and slammed the door on her, forcing her to choke back the rest of her sentence.

He drove away, leaving her literally to eat the dust he had churned up beneath the tyres of his Land Rover, and she stamped her foot in a fit of frustration and rage before she untethered Pegasus and leapt on to his back to ride to the river camp.

Her Brahman heifers were back where they belonged when she arrived there, and a team of workers from Izilwane were already working on the fence to repair the damage. There was no sign, however, of the impala, the small antelope with reddish gold coat and white underparts. They had obviously scattered, leaping the fences with their remarkable grace and agility to find grazing in one of her many other camps.

The sound of an approaching horse made Frances turn in the saddle. It was Tony, and he was surveying the scene of activity in the river camp with raised eyebrows.

'It looks as if you've got problems,' he remarked when he reined his horse in beside hers.

'You can say that again!' she replied angrily. 'Some idiot cut the fence, and the result was an unpleasant display of fireworks between Byron Rockford and myself.'

'I'm sorry to hear that.' His eyes were narrowed against the glare of the sun while he studied her intently. 'Have you any idea who did the damage?'

'No idea at all,' she shook her head, and an angry frown creased her brow when she caught a glimpse of Byron Rockford joining the team of workers repairing the fence.

'These things do happen occasionally,' Tony tried to console her, his hand gripping her shoulder at the very moment Byron chose to look up and glance their way. 'Don't let this incident upset you,' Tony added.

'I shall try not to,' she said and, aware of those tawny eyes observing them from the other side of the fence, she turned her head and smiled warmly at Tony.

Let Byron Rockford make whatever he chooses of that!

'I believe you had a bit of drama here today,' Megan remarked when they were relaxing in the lounge after dinner that evening.

'That's putting it mildly!' snorted Frances, laying down her book and stretching her long, shapely legs out in front of her. 'And I can guess who told you.'

'It wasn't Byron, if that's what you're thinking.' Megan paused in the process of sewing a button on to one of her blouses and looked up, her blue gaze meeting Frances'. 'Jack Harriman, one of the wardens, came into the curio shop today, and it was he who told me what had happened.'

Frances accepted this information with a slightly apologetic twitch of her lips, and Megan lowered her gaze to resume her sewing while Frances continued to observe her cousin without actually seeing her. Her mind was lingering on the unfortunate incident which had occurred that day, and she was wondering . . .!

'Do you have any idea who might have cut the fence?' Megan asked as if she had intercepted Frances' thoughts.

'I have no idea whatsoever,' Frances frowned angrily, 'but I was accused of committing that offence in order to lure the animals on to my land so that I could hunt them down whenever I felt the whim for it, and I'm quoting Byron Rockford almost verbatim.'

'Oh, Frances, he was angry and upset, and I'm sure he didn't mean that! When you know him better——'

'I have no desire to know him better, thank you very much!' Frances interrupted her cousin sharply, picking up her book to continue reading, and flinging it aside again seconds later. 'If ever I have reason to regret buying Thorndale it will be because of that man's despicable arrogance, his conceit, and the unfounded accusations I've been forced to endure!'

'Give the man a break, Frances,' Megan pleaded in his defence. 'He's worked exceptionally hard to bring the game park up to its present standard, and if you were in his position you might have reacted in exactly the same way he did today.'

'I might have,' Frances conceded thoughtfully, trying to place herself in Byron's position as she had done so charitably that morning, but she could still not forgive him entirely. 'Oh, let's face it, Megan—Byron Rockford and I simply rub each other up the wrong way, and I doubt if that will ever change.'

Megan studied her in silence, her glance sliding over the tall, slender body reclining in the chair. Frances had changed into a creamy silk dress before dinner that evening, and her dark, lustrous hair had been left free of its usual confinement to cascade on to smooth, tanned shoulders. Frances was totally unaware of her appearance, but at that moment her femininity made her an unlikely candidate for the profession she had chosen.

'You're actually similar in many ways,' Megan observed in her quiet, calm voice.

'God forbid!' Frances snorted disparagingly.

'But it's true!' insisted Megan. 'You're both strong in body and in spirit with a wilful determination to succeed, and you're not afraid to work hard for what you want. It's only natural that there'll be a few sparks when two similar forces meet.'

'Two similar forces,' Frances echoed thoughtfully, shaking her head. She was neither arrogant nor conceited, and she had never accused anyone unjustly. Well . . . not until today, at least, and then it had been in retaliation to Byron's accusation that she had cut the fence for an objectionable purpose. She could forgive him on the basis that he did not know her very well, but it still hurt that he could think . . .! *Dammit*, did it really matter what he thought of her? 'I'm going to bed,' she announced abruptly, getting to her feet. 'I've had a rough day, I'm tired, and I'm beginning to see things in myself that I don't like.'

Megan rose as well, and they left the lounge, switching off the lights as they went.

'Sleep well, Frances,' Megan had said when they went to their separate rooms, but Frances did *not* sleep well.

She tossed and turned for several hours, thinking about Byron Rockford and the existing situation between them. She tried to think of Tony. He was nice, easy-going and friendly, but Byron's granite-hard features continued to intrude. A 'young fool', that was what Byron had called Tony, and from that alone she could gather that the relationship between them, as neighbours, had been as rocky as the present relationship between Byron and herself.

Two similar forces! Megan's words bounced through Frances' mind, and she almost laughed out loud at the thought. She had never yet made a habit of deliberately antagonising people, but Byron seemed to thrive on it. Byron and herself? Two similar forces? *Never!*

CHAPTER FOUR

MEGAN celebrated her twenty-first birthday a few weeks later with a *braai* on the Saturday evening at her parents' home in Louisville. The weather was perfect for an outdoor party, and several guests were already seated round the barbecue in Aunt Vivien's and Uncle Peter's beautiful, well-lit garden when Frances arrived with Tony.

Among many of the familiar faces Frances caught a glimpse of her uncle's partner, Dr Dane Trafford, with his wife Dr Jessica Neal, and their two small sons. Since her marriage to Dr Trafford, Dr Neal had relinquished her regular practice to help as a locum in Louisville while she reared her children, and she was extremely well liked and respected, as a doctor and also as a person. It was Dr Neal who had brought Frances' brother and sister into the world, and Frances knew that Olivia still preferred to consult Dr Neal, whenever it was necessary, rather than her sister-in-law's husband, Peter O'Brien.

Frances' father and stepmother were also at the party with Logan and Janet, and the two children stormed down upon Frances, almost knocking her down with their exuberant welcome.

'May we go back to Thorndale with you this evening?' they demanded almost simultaneously, and the seven-year-old Janet, with her father's dark hair and her mother's delicate features, bounced up and down excitedly in front of Frances.

'If Mom and Dad will let you,' Frances agreed, glancing at Bernard and Olivia, who had barely been given the opportunity to greet her properly.

'You can't go out to the farm with Frances when you haven't got pyjamas, or even a toothbrush with you,'

59

Olivia remonstrated gently with the two children.

'Oh, but we have!' insisted Logan, the tall and sturdy ten-year-old with his father's strong features and his mother's auburn hair. 'We brought them along just in case, and they're in the car.'

'Is that so?' Olivia exchanged an amused glance with her husband before she added, 'Well, in that case I should imagine it depends on whether or not Frances wants you on the farm with her.'

'Can we, Frances? Can we come with you?' the two children chorused anxiously.

'Of course you may come home with me this evening,' Frances agreed laughingly, but her expression sobered as she glanced at Tony. 'You don't object to having two extra passengers when we leave here later this evening, do you?'

'I have no objections at all,' Tony assured her, flashing the smile that had the ability to quicken the pace of a woman's heart, but Frances' pulse rate remained unaffected.

The fires had been lit, and wood-smoke was curling into the warm night air when Frances left Tony in the company of her father and Olivia while she went in search of Megan, and she was still wishing her cousin a happy birthday a few minutes later when she felt an odd sensation shifting up and down her spine.

'Hello, Byron, I'm so glad you could come,' Megan smiled warmly, glancing beyond Frances, and Frances closed her eyes briefly. She should have known!

Frances moved aside as Byron stepped forward with a gift-wrapped package in his hands. 'Happy twenty-first birthday, Megan.'

'Thank you, Byron.' Megan had to stand on her toes and draw his head down to plant a kiss on his rugged cheek. 'And thank you for the gift.'

'My pleasure,' he smiled, but his smile was no more than a polite grimace when he turned to meet Frances' dark, cool glance. 'Good evening, Frances.'

'Good evening,' she responded stiffly, a part of her admitting treacherously that he looked magnificent in his grey slacks, impeccably tailored blue blazer and white open-necked shirt.

'It has been some weeks since our last unfortunate meeting,' he remarked with a hint of mockery in his tawny gaze.

'So it has,' Frances agreed coolly, her mind racing in its search for an adequate reason to make a quick and polite exit, but her cousin forestalled her.

'Would you excuse me?' Megan smiled apologetically. 'I think my mother needs my help with the salads and the glasses.'

She was gone before her cousin could formulate a valid excuse to accompany her and, left alone with Byron, Frances felt stiff and awkward for the first time in his company.

'Did you come to the party on your own this evening?' he asked, his narrowed glance flicking over her, taking in every detail of her appearance in the floral silk dress with its slender shoulder straps, and lingering with a strange intensity on the gold pendant in the shape of a heart which had been a gift from Olivia and her father some years ago on her birthday.

'I came with Tony,' she said bluntly.

'I see.' His expression was shuttered as he lowered his tawny gaze once again to the heart-shaped pendant nestling against her smooth skin, where the shadowy cleft between her breasts was only just visible above the loose-fitting bodice of her dress, and for some peculiar reason she felt her heartbeat quicken to send an embarrassing warmth flowing into her cheeks. 'How are my impala doing on your farm?' he questioned her mockingly.

'Wonderfully, I'm sure. Nor have they diminished in number since I haven't yet had the whim to go hunting,' she replied caustically, that unfathomable anger flaring inside her and setting fire to her eyes. 'If you'll excuse me,

Mr Rockford, I think I've left my escort alone long enough.'

She left him standing beneath the shallow terrace steps, and walked back to where Tony was waiting for her, but she could feel Byron's eyes burning into her back with every step she took.

She did her best to ignore him, but at odd times during the evening she found herself glancing in his direction while she was mingling with the guests. Peter O'Brien, tall, lean and fair, had stood with his wife, Vivien, at his side when he had made his speech before handing a blushing Megan the traditional key to the door and, with the formalities over, everyone could relax and enjoy themselves. The men had grouped themselves round the open fire, talking and joking and drinking beer while the meat was being roasted on the red-hot coals. Frances noticed that Byron was at ease and relaxed in their company, and . . . *dammit*, it was annoying to find that she could not prevent herself from staring so frequently in his direction.

'I couldn't help noticing that you were talking to Byron Rockford earlier this evening.' Tony drew Frances' attention away from the lively conversation among the group of young people they were both acquainted with.

'Yes, I was talking to him,' she answered casually, not wanting to dwell on the brief verbal altercation between Byron and herself, but Tony was strangely persistent.

'What were you talking about?' he asked, and she found his prying into her conversation with Byron vaguely annoying.

'Oh, he wanted to know how his impala were doing on my farm,' she answered airily, and with a hint of sarcasm in her voice, then she took his hand and pulled him up out of his chair. 'Come on, Tony, let's go and help ourselves to something to eat. I'm starving, and that meat smells delicious.'

Tony did not persist with his queries, but he lapsed into a strangely sombre mood which seemed to abate only when the dancing started later that evening.

Recorded music was relayed out into the garden with its smooth lawn, and Frances had danced several times with Tony when they decided to take a break to sit and watch the others swaying across the lawn in time to the music. Frances could not help noticing that Byron had danced with Megan as well as Olivia and Aunt Vivien, and the music had changed to a slow waltz when she suddenly saw him striding in her direction with a purposeful look on his rugged face.

'Let's dance, Tony,' Frances suggested hastily to escape having to dance with Byron, and Tony did not need a second invitation.

He drew her eagerly into his arms and, when he twirled her round in time to the music, she caught a brief glimpse of Byron Rockford observing them from a distance with one heavy eyebrow raised in sardonic amusement before he turned away.

'You're very beautiful, Frances,' Tony murmured unexpectedly, his arm tightening about her waist, 'and I think I'm falling in love with you.'

Frances was inwardly amused when she eased herself away from him with a firm hand against his shoulder. 'Do you know what I think?'

'What?' he smiled into her dark eyes, which were on a level with his.

'I think you should stop talking and concentrate on dancing.'

Tony laughed softly and tried once again to draw her closer to him, but Frances did not ease the pressure of her hand against his shoulder, and he grimaced playfully as he reluctantly slackened the grip of the arm he had about her waist.

As the evening wore on Frances managed to have a few words alone with her father, and she was asking his advice about the culling of her herd of Afrikaner cattle when Byron Rockford intruded on their conversation.

'May I dance with your daughter, Mr King?'

'Certainly you may,' Bernard King announced with a hint of laughter in his eyes at the look of helpless resignation that flashed across Frances' rigid face.

On this occasion she was not given the opportunity to escape him. Byron held out his large hand, and Frances slipped hers into it. She felt the warm roughness of his palm against the soft pads of her fingers, and an electrified sensation shot up her arm to brush across quivering, receptive nerve ends. She was shaken and on edge when Byron drew her towards the dancing couples on the lawn, and it took a considerable amount of self-control not to flinch away from that broad hand resting lightly against the hollow of her back. His touch was strangely disturbing, and his nearness seemed to set off an alarm inside her, alerting her to something which she could not grasp for the moment.

'It's quite a party,' he remarked while they moved across the smooth lawn in time to the slow, rhythmic throbbing of the music, and Frances was surprised to discover that, for a man of his size, Byron was light on his feet.

'Since you're not much of a socialiser, I didn't think you would be capable of drawing comparisons,' she responded sarcastically.

'If I've given the impression that I'm more at home among the animals in the game park than among people, then I shall have to do something about remedying that incorrect image people have of me,' he laughed shortly, ignoring her sarcasm.

'Does it bother you what people think about you?' she asked, trying desperately to cope with the unfamiliar sensations aroused by the nearness of his male body.

'No, it doesn't really,' he shook his head.

'I didn't think it would.'

He lowered his gaze to meet hers, and raised a quizzical eyebrow. 'You make me sound quite nasty!'

'Aren't you?'

'I walked into that one, didn't I,' he observed, the low

rumble of his laughter pleasing on the ear, and making her wish that he would laugh like that more often. 'I must tell you that you're looking exceptionally lovely this evening, Frances,' he complimented her unexpectedly.

'Oh, you like my dress, do you?' she responded sarcastically. 'I guess it does make a change from the dirty old working clothes you've always seen me in, but then we're fortunately not in the habit of socialising together very often.'

His expression became shuttered, but his tawny gaze drew hers, and held it compellingly. 'You don't like me, do you?'

'No, I don't,' she answered him bluntly, seeing no reason why she should hide the fact that she disliked him intensely.

'I like honesty,' he admitted, his expression hardening and, when the music stopped, he let his arm fall away from her, but the grip of his hand tightened on hers. 'Perhaps I can oblige you by giving you reason to dislike me even more.'

'Let go of me!' she snapped through her teeth when he pulled her into the deep shadows beneath the trees in the spacious garden. 'Let go, do you hear?'

'Not yet, Frances! Not yet!' he announced harshly, pulling her deeper into the shadows to where they would not be seen by the rest of the guests.

Frances tried to wrench her hand from his, but his fingers tightened in a punishing grip that almost made her cry out in agony when he halted abruptly in his stride behind the broad stem of an old oak tree which made her recall the many times she and Megan had played hide-and-seek in that very garden as children.

'What are you——' she began, but she lost her breath along with her voice when muscled arms whipped about her like steel cords, crushing her slender body against a hard, masculine frame, and a very male mouth descended on hers, bruising her untutored lips until they were forced apart beneath his to lend an unwanted intimacy to this equally unwanted experience.

Frances had never been kissed before by anyone other than the members of her family and, unlike most girls, being kissed by a man was not something she had fantasised about, but she would never have dreamed that it could be such an earth-shattering experience. Her breasts were hurting against Byron's hard chest, and her heart was racing, sending the flow of blood through her veins at a dizzying pace until there was an odd soaring in her ears. She forced her hands between them in an attempt to push him away, but Byron was as solid and immovable as a concrete wall, and his kiss seemed to go on for ever, the pressure of his mouth easing to move against hers with a sensuality that demanded and finally received a response from her lips which came almost as naturally as breathing.

Through the cotton of his shirt she could feel the warmth and dampness of his skin against her palms. His heart was thudding beneath her fingers, and touching him like that sent a liquid warmth flowing through her body that relaxed her taut muscles until she was soft and pliant in his arms.

God, what's happening to me? she wondered frantically. I'm not supposed to enjoy this, I'm supposed to be hating every minute of it!

The thought had barely skipped through her mind when she was released as abruptly as she had been taken, and she felt herself swaying like a sapling in the cool darkness without the support of Byron's strong arms about her. She was aware that she was breathing jerkily while she tried to read his expression, but it was too dark to see more than the blur of his rugged features, and perhaps it was just as well that neither of them could see each other's faces at that moment.

'You may be a cattle rancher, Frances, but you're a woman first,' his low, harsh voice grated along nerves which were unexpectedly raw and tender, 'and next time you want to pick a fight, I suggest you choose someone who isn't afraid to cross swords with you!'

He turned on his heel, striding away from her, and leaving her there in the protective shadow of the trees with a flaming face and a body that was trembling so much she had to lean against the stem of the oak for support.

Frances was, at first, too shaken by the feelings Byron had aroused in her to be angered by his behaviour, and it was only when she had succeeded in regaining her composure that she was engulfed in a storm of rage. How dared he do that to her! How dared he kiss her, and—and——! Oh, God, she did not even want to think about her own reaction to his kisses!

'Byron left rather suddenly,' Megan whispered to Frances shortly after Frances had scraped together sufficient courage to emerge from the shadow of the trees to face everyone, and Byron in particular. 'I wonder why?' Megan murmured curiously.

'Perhaps his socialising ability had been stretched to its maximum,' Frances announced bitingly despite the wave of relief that washed over her, and she was aware of Megan's faintly startled glance following her when she walked away to where Tony was waiting for her with a vaguely petulant look on his handsome face.

It was eleven o'clock that evening when Frances and Tony decided to leave the party with Logan and Janet, who climbed sleepily, but nevertheless excitedly, into the back of Tony's red BMW.

'We'll fetch the children tomorrow afternoon,' Olivia told Frances when they had said good night.

'Why not come for lunch and spend the afternoon with me?' suggested Frances. 'We haven't seen much of each other in recent weeks, and it would be nice to have my family with me for a few hours.'

'I'd like that very much,' Olivia smiled, 'but I shall have to speak to your father first. I'll give you a call early tomorrow morning. Would that be okay?'

'That would be fine,' Frances agreed, kissing Olivia's cheek before she got into the car. 'I'll see you tomorrow, then.'

The drive to Thorndale took twenty minutes, and two sleepy children stumbled out of the car with Frances and Tony when he had parked his car close to the entrance of the house. Major had bounded on to the verandah, and he was panting excitedly with the attention he was receiving from the children while Frances unlocked the door and switched on the light in the hall.

'Thanks for taking me this evening,' she said, turning to Tony when he followed them inside.

'It was my pleasure,' he announced, glancing at Logan and Janet, who hovered close to Frances with Major between them, their eyes glued inquisitively on the faces of the adults.

Frances sensed that Tony wanted to be alone with her, but one close encounter with a man that evening had been more than enough, and she was not in the mood for another, especially not with Tony, who had begun to take their relationship much too seriously lately for her liking.

'Good night, Tony.'

Frances held out her hand, aware of two very disappointed faces who had obviously expected to witness a kiss, at the very least, but they were not entirely disappointed. Tony took the hand she had offered him, and he had carried it to his lips before Frances could stop him.

'Good night, Frances,' he smiled, releasing her hand, and then he was gone, closing the door behind him.

'Is he your boy-friend?' Logan wanted to know when Frances showed him to his room, and a smile plucked at Frances' mouth.

'No, he's just a friend.'

'I like Mr Rockford,' Janet lisped through the gap in her front teeth.

'Oh, do you?' Frances remarked drily, shutting her mind to the memory of what had occurred between

Byron and herself earlier that evening.

'He said he would take us for a drive through his game park in the morning to see the animals,' announced Janet, and Frances felt her insides jerk.

'Did he indeed?' she muttered, hiding her anger behind an outwardly calm expression when she opened the door to the room Logan would sleep in.

'Frances?' Janet tugged at Frances' hand. 'Can I sleep with you?'

'Sure, baby,' Frances smiled down at her little sister, then she glanced at her young brother who was quite happy to have a room to himself. 'The bathroom is down the passage, Logan, and don't forget to brush your teeth before you go to bed.'

'I won't forget,' Logan promised. 'Good night, Frances. Good night, Janet.'

They said good night, and Frances put Major out of the kitchen door before she took Janet along to her own room. The three-quarter-sized bed was big enough for both of them, and it was not long before Frances slid between the sheets with Janet's small body lying close to hers. There was nothing strange about having her little sister in bed with her; it had been quite a regular occurrence in past years when she had come home for the holidays, but on this particular night Frances was still lying awake long after Janet had gone to sleep.

She did not want to think of the way Byron had kissed her, but it all came rushing back to her with a stunning clarity that made her tremble at the mere memory of it. Oh, *damn*! She wished Byron had not done that! She felt confused and bewildered, but most of all she was filled with an anger which she could not explain even to herself. And tomorrow . . . ! She did not want to think about tomorrow, but she had to. Byron had promised the children that he would take them for a drive through the game park, and she would have to accompany them, unless she could think up a good enough excuse not to, but she had a feeling that *any* excuse would be considered cowardly. She could be called many things, such as stubborn, determined, and sometimes short-tempered, but no one could ever accuse her of being a coward.

Oh, lord! If only the sun would take its time in rising in the morning to give her more of a chance to prepare herself for having to face Byron again!

'Mr Rockford's here! Mr Rockford's here!' Janet exclaimed, her brown eyes alight with excitement when she stormed out of the house on the Sunday morning at the sound of a Land Rover approaching, and Major bounded out after her with Logan following at a calmer pace, but with no less excitement.

Byron was getting out of the Land Rover when Frances stepped on to the verandah, and her insides tightened oddly at the sight of him. His brown slacks hugged his lean hips and muscular thighs, and his cream-coloured shirt seemed to fit too tightly across the width of his massive chest and shoulders. That aura of raw masculinity which always surrounded him appealed to her senses and, despite her attempts to the contrary, she was forced to admit to herself that there was something about Byron Rockford that attracted her.

'Hello, Janet, and you look so pretty this morning,' Byron was saying, making Janet giggle shyly, then he glanced at the tall boy approaching him and held out his hand. 'Hello, Logan.'

'Good morning, Mr Rockford,' Logan addressed him in a very adult manner while they shook hands, then Byron glanced up, and his sensuous mouth tightened perceptibly when he saw Frances standing below the verandah steps.

Frances' glance was unwavering, her expression cool, but she was never quite sure afterwards how she had succeeded in sustaining his gaze without blushing at the memory of their last encounter.

'Why don't you two get into the Land Rover?' Byron

suggested to the children. 'I'd like a private word with your sister before we leave.'

'Okay,' they agreed readily, and he opened the door for them to scramble into the back of the vehicle while he approached Frances with those long, determined strides which were becoming so familiar to her.

At close range his expression was hard, and his tawny gaze impersonal when it met hers. 'I know you're not partial to my company, you've made that quite clear, but this outing was arranged last night before——'

'You don't have to explain,' Frances interrupted him coldly, 'and I have no intention of spoiling the outing for Logan and Janet by refusing to go with you.'

He nodded curtly. 'I appreciate your understanding.'

Byron strode back to the Land Rover without waiting for her, and Frances followed him after giving an abrupt command to Major when he had wanted to accompany her. She got in beside Byron, gathering together the wide skirt of her grey and white striped summer frock before she closed the door.

'All set?' asked Byron, turning his head to glance into the back of the Land Rover.

'Yes!' Janet and Logan chorused.

The drive from Thorndale to the game park took only a few minutes. Byron raised his hand to acknowledge the salute of the black security officer at the gate, and a few seconds later they turned off to the left, taking a clearly marked route through the park.

Frances was a silent passenger, but she was annoyingly aware of the man seated beside her. His rugged profile was stern, and his brown hair, trimmed neatly into his neck, had a tendency to curl about his ears and on to his broad forehead. There were laughter lines about his eyes, but she found herself wondering cynically if he ever really laughed.

'Oh, look, there's a giraffe!' Janet's cry of excitement intruded on her thoughts.

'And there are at least ten more!' added Logan,

leaning over Janet and pointing in the direction where a herd of long-necked giraffe were browsing amongst the trees.

'The giraffe has the keenest sight of all the game animals in Africa, and its height naturally allows it to have a far better view,' Byron explained, reducing speed.

'What is its life expectancy? Frances asked with interest, incapable of maintaining her determined silence as she leaned towards Byron to view the tall, somewhat ungainly animals through the window on his side, and he turned his head abruptly, his tawny glance colliding with hers for a brief moment, but it had been quite sufficient to make her pulses leap a little wildly.

'The giraffe has been known to live up to twenty-eight years in captivity,' he answered her query, driving on past the animals and increasing speed slightly.

During the next fifteen minutes they saw a herd of springbok very briefly before the sleek-bodied animals darted away amongst the trees and the tall grass, but they had not gone much farther when Byron turned off the road and parked the Land Rover beneath an acacia tree.

'Why are we stopping?' Janet asked inquisitively, leaning over the back of Byron's seat.

'Look straight ahead of you, Janet,' he said, pointing towards a clearing amongst the trees where zebra, wildebeest, eland and impala were grazing together contentedly.

'Could we get out and walk closer?' Logan asked in a lowered voice, as if he was afraid that the animals might hear him and scatter.

'Sure,' Byron agreed, 'but only if you stay close to me.'

They all got out of the Land Rover, leaving the doors open as Byron instructed, and following him through the tall grass towards the acacia trees ahead of them from where they would have a much clearer view of the animals.

The cicadas were shrilling loudly in the blazing heat of the morning when Byron gestured them silently into the shade of the acacia trees. They were so close to the animals that they could have struck one if they had thrown a pebble in its direction, and they stood in silence, watching the zebra moving in amongst the wildebeest, and holding their breath almost in awe when the impala moved away to give them a clearer view of the herd of eland with their spirally twisted horns and their pale fawn coats with the few white body stripes.

'An eland bull can weigh up to five hundred and forty-four kilograms,' whispered Byron, standing directly behind Frances so that his body heat penetrated the cotton of her frock while the faint smell of his masculine cologne did strange things to her senses. 'It's a curious thing,' he added, 'but you'll notice that the cows have longer horns than the bulls.'

Frances was looking, but she was not seeing anything. She was aware only of the man standing behind her, and she was also very much aware of the strange way her own body was beginning to react to his nearness.

'It's time to move on,' Byron said after a few minutes, and the children, their faces glowing with wonder, returned to the Land Rover with some reluctance.

It took yet another hour before they reached the fenced-in area of the camp with its thatch-roofed bungalows nestling against the side of the hill amongst the mopani, jacaranda and baobab trees. Byron drove past the main building with its offices, shops, restaurant and recreation rooms. Beyond this building there was a pool surrounded by tables and colourful umbrellas where visitors could cool off in the heat, and Frances almost envied Megan for having her curio shop in these picturesque surroundings.

'How about something cold to drink?' Byron asked when he parked his Land Rover in front of one of the larger bungalows in the camp.

'Yes, please!' Logan and Janet answered simultaneously when they got out of the Land Rover, and

followed him into the lounge of the cool bungalow with
its comfortable cane bench and chairs and woven rugs on
the tiled floor.

There was a portable television set on a table in the
corner of the room, but it was unplugged, and looked as if
it was seldom used. His hi-fi equipment was impressive
with several records stashed neatly into one of its
compartments, and there was a bookcase filled with
books. There was also a zebra skin hanging against one
of the walls, and it made Frances shudder inwardly to
think that he might have shot the animal for that purpose
alone.

'I've got orange juice, freshly squeezed and ice-cold,
and then there's lemonade and Coke,' Byron ticked off
on his fingers the liquid contents of his refrigerator.
'What will you have?'

'Orange juice, please,' lisped Janet, and Logan echoed
that request.

'What about you, Frances?'

Frances turned from examining a watercolour painting of a kudu which she had recognised as Megan's work.
'I'll have the same, thank you.'

'Sit down,' Byron invited, smiling faintly as if he was
aware of that inner resentment she was nursing at having
to accept his hospitality. 'Make yourselves comfortable.'

They were left alone in his lounge while he went into
the kitchen, and he returned moments later with a jug of
orange juice and glasses on a tray. The ice tinkled in the
jug when he poured its contents into the four glasses, and
the children helped themselves, but he brought Frances
her glass of orange juice and, to her chagrin, seated
himself in the chair beside her own.

'Is this your home, Mr Rockford?' asked Logan, his
grey, steady glance meeting Byron's while they drank the
refreshing fruit juice.

'If one could call it a home, yes,' Byron smiled,
stretching his long legs comfortably in front of him and

taking a long drink out of his glass. 'It has one bedroom, a bathroom, a kitchen, and this lounge. It's not much, but it's very comfortable.'

'Don't you have a dining-room?' Janet asked with the concern of a born housewife.

'No, I eat in the kitchen, or I eat in the restaurant after everyone else has had their meal.'

A picture of loneliness was taking shape in Frances' mind. Was Byron lonely? She pulled her thoughts up sharply and glanced at her watch. Eleven-thirty! The morning had flown!

'If you don't mind, we really must leave,' she announced and, draining her glass, rose to place it on the tray he had left on the low table between the bench and the chairs.

'Oh, must we?' the children asked, looking as reluctant as they sounded to leave Izilwane and return to Thorndale.

'I'm expecting Mom and Dad at the farm in half an hour's time, and I'd hate not to be there when they arrive,' Frances explained.

'Frances is right. It's time I took you back to the farm,' Byron supported her, draining his own glass and rising to his feet. 'Come on, let's go.'

They were walking past the wall where the zebra skin had been hung when Byron said, 'I didn't shoot the zebra simply for the skin. It was caught in a poacher's snare some years ago, and the animal was so badly injured that we had no option but to put it out of its misery. The two black game guards who worked directly under me had the skin cured, and they gave it to me as a gift.'

Frances looked up sharply to encounter the mocking appraisal of Byron's tawny eyes, but she looked away again hastily, too astounded to say anything. Had he, in some uncanny way, guessed her thoughts about the zebra skin, or had he merely mentioned it as a matter of interest? She could not decide which it was, and she was too shaken to question him about it. A verbal battle with this man was one thing, but it was quite something else if he was developing the ability to read her mind.

CHAPTER FIVE

BERNARD and Olivia King arrived at Thorndale shortly after Byron had parked his Land Rover beneath the shady jacaranda trees, and Frances had never been more relieved to see anyone. A few minutes in Byron Rockford's company had been quite sufficient in the past, but having to cope with his disturbing presence for two hours had left her nerves in unpleasant knots.

'Don't be in such a hurry to return to Izilwane, Byron,' Olivia objected when Byron was about to take his leave of them. 'Stay and chat for a while.'

'Well, I . . .'

His tawny gaze settled on Frances, placing her in the awkward position where she felt obliged to say, 'You're welcome to stay, if you wish.'

'Thank you, I will stay, but only for a few minutes,' he smiled with a hint of mockery in his glance, and Frances was annoyingly convinced that he knew exactly how she felt.

They went into the house, seeking refuge from the heat, and Frances led the way into the lounge, which had now been cleared of the dining-room suite to create a restful, uncluttered appearance. The atmosphere was relaxed with her family around her, but that did not rid her entirely of that awful tension which was gripping her insides as she watched her parents respond to Byron's particular brand of charm. She knew that her father was not a man who suffered fools gladly, but Byron was not a fool, and Frances suspected that this was why there was such an easy relationship between her father and the man she still found herself disliking intensely at times.

Frances did not join in the conversation. She sat, instead, and watched the minutes lengthen into an hour,

until she was once again obliged to invite Byron to stay to
lunch. If she had hoped that he would refuse her
invitation, then she was disappointed. He accepted with
that hint of mockery in his smile which only she seemed
to notice and, as a result, she sat fuming silently
throughout lunch that Sunday. She had begun to dread
the rest of the afternoon, but Byron left immediately after
lunch, and Frances was so relieved that she sagged into a
chair in the lounge, sighing heavily.

Her father went for a walk, taking Logan and Janet
with him, and the silence that descended on the house
was beginning to soothe her ruffled nerves when she
looked up to find Olivia observing her with a curious
expression in her grey eyes.

'May I ask you something, Frances?'

'Fire away,' she smiled, stretching her long, shapely
legs in front of her and leaning back comfortably in her
chair.

'You're not still angry with Byron because of what
happened that very first day you came here to Thorndale,
are you?'

The query was unexpected, but there had always been
complete honesty between Frances and Olivia, and on
this occasion, like all the rest, Frances did not withhold
the truth.

'Yes, I am,' she said, her striking features tightening
with the extent of her feelings. 'I'm angry about that, and
about several other things which have happened since
then.'

'Such as?' Olivia probed, then a faintly apologetic
smile curved her soft mouth. 'Or am I prying into
something which doesn't concern me?'

Frances stared at the small, slender woman with the
soft auburn curls framing her delicate features, and a
warmth invaded her heart. Olivia was a youthful thirty-
nine, and sixteen years Frances' senior, but the age
difference had never hampered their relationship.
Frances had been ten and Olivia twenty-six when they

had first met, but from that very first meeting there had been an indefinable bond between them which had grown and strengthened over the years, and not once had Frances regretted the fact that her father had married this woman. Olivia had come into their lives at a time when she had been most needed, and with her warm, gentle and compassionate nature she had made their house at Mountain View a home again.

There was a glimmer of tears in Frances' dark eyes when she crossed the room quickly to sit beside Olivia on the sofa.

'I doubt if my own mother could have meant as much to me as you do, Olivia,' she confessed, taking her stepmother's small and capable hands into her own. 'You've been everything I could ever have wanted in a mother, but, best of all, you've been my friend, my very dear friend, and for that reason I've never considered that you're prying when you question me about something.'

'Thank you, darling.' There was a tender warmth in Olivia's smile, and a hint of tears in her eyes when she leaned forward to kiss Frances lightly on the cheek. 'That's the nicest thing you've said to me in a long time.'

'But you've always known that that's how I felt, haven't you, Olivia?'

'Yes, I have,' whispered Olivia, 'and I love you for it.'

They embraced, and the gravity of the moment was lightened when they laughed away their tears.

'To get back to Byron Rockford,' Frances said at length, her mouth tightening with displeasure. 'Why is it that some men can be so conceited and arrogant when a woman invades what they consider to be their territory, while others have the ability to accept it as something quite natural?'

'Darling, there are very few men who take kindly to a woman invading their territory,' Olivia explained wisely, but with a humorous twinkle in her eyes. 'Some are tolerant and accept the invasion in silence, while others are not afraid to make their displeasure known, and I gather Byron is one of the latter.'

'You gather correctly,' Frances nodded, her mouth curving in a cynical smile. 'He's convinced I'm not going to make a success of farming, and he's quite sure I shall be wanting to sell before the end of the year.'

'Oh, dear!' Olivia's smile conveyed her familiarity with Frances' capabilities and determination. 'You'll simply have to prove him wrong, won't you?'

'That's something I shall take a great delight in doing, believe me!' Frances laughed mirthlessly, glancing up at the portrait of George Wilkins, and she could almost swear that she glimpsed a look of approval in his watery grey eyes.

Frances spent the following week culling her Afrikaner cattle. It was a mammoth task having to grade and sort them into different camps depending on their age and condition. She had to decide which to sell and which to retain, and it was, at times, a difficult decision which required her father's expert advice. Mountain View, her father's cattle ranch, was stocked with the most sought-after Afrikaner cattle in the district, and Frances was determined that Thorndale would one day be classed a close second with Afrikaner as well as Brahman cattle.

She was up at six-thirty on the Thursday morning of that same week, drinking a cup of coffee in the kitchen with Megan, when she saw Sipho racing towards the house on horseback, and she knew instantly that something was wrong.

'*Nkosazana!*' he exclaimed anxiously and without dismounting when she stepped outside. '*Ucingo lunqanyuliwe!*'

'Not again!' Frances sighed angrily. 'Where was the fence cut this time?'

'The same place, *Nkosazana.*'

'*Damn!*' she muttered furiously, her features tightening at the mere thought of the accusations she would have to endure once again. 'Round up some of the herdsmen, Sipho. I'll take the jeep and meet you at the river camp.'

'*Yebo, Nkosazana*,' he nodded, tugging at the reins to turn his sweating horse and galloping away at the same breakneck speed as he had arrived.

'Do me a favour, Megan.' Frances turned to her cousin with a frown creasing her brow. 'Please give Byron a call and tell him what's happened.'

Frances did not wait to see whether Megan carried out the instruction she had given her. She ran towards the shed where the jeep was kept, and a few minutes later she was speeding along the bumpy tracks towards the river camp where she kept her herd of Brahman.

Frances arrived at the camp within less than ten minutes, and she stared incredulously at the fence, which had been cut in such a way that it curled aside like two badly made Swiss rolls to leave a gaping opening where an animal as large as an eland could wander through without difficulty. Her herd of Brahman were all accounted for, and the damage had been discovered early enough in the morning to give her reason to hope that Byron would be able to say the same about the animals in his game park, but . . .!

Her thoughts halted abruptly, and she lowered herself on to her haunches near the fence. There were hoof-prints in the dew-wet earth. They could have been made by Sipho's horse, or her own for that matter, and there was no sense in allowing herself to think differently. The hoof-prints were not fresh, they could have been made the day before, and any one of her herdsmen could have been there. It was a logical thought, but it niggled.

Sipho arrived with the herdsmen on their horses, and Frances was still on her haunches, studying the hoof-prints, when Byron arrived in his Land Rover. Directly behind him was a truck bringing a team of workers to repair the fence, and Frances rose slowly when Byron got out of his Land Rover to walk with long strides towards the fence. She braced herself mentally for his verbal attack, but he acknowledged her presence with a curt nod, and maintained a stony silence while he inspected the damage done to the fence.

'I know what you're thinking, Byron Rockford!' she wanted to shout at him. 'You think I cut the fence, so why don't you just say it, and be done with it?'

She could cope with his anger and his accusations, but she could not cope with his silence. It gnawed away at her nerves until they felt frayed and raw, and frustration added fire to the anger which was building up inside her.

'*Kufanele sithole onqamula ucingo,*' Sipho interrupted her thoughts, and she made a determined effort to pull herself together.

'Yes, Sipho,' she agreed, her mouth tightening with renewed anger, and something else which she could not define at that moment when she saw Byron's khaki-clad figure striding back towards the Land Rover. 'We must find the one who cuts the fence,' she repeated Sipho's statement absently.

Dammit! If only Byron had said something to her instead of maintaining such a morose silence.

'*Umlungu Omkhulu* is very angry,' remarked the *Induna*, his eyes shaded beneath the brim of his hat when his glance followed the Land Rover as it drove away at speed.

'So am I, Sipho,' admitted Frances, thrusting her fingers into the hip pockets of her faded denims, and frowning down at the hoof-prints in the soft earth. 'This is the second time the fence has been cut, and I'd give anything to know *who* did it, and *why*.'

She stayed there only a few minutes longer to watch the proceedings, then she got into her jeep and drove back to the house where Gladys was waiting for her to serve breakfast.

Sipho made discreet enquiries during the next few days, but to no avail. When Tony heard what had happened he had willingly agreed to make a few enquiries of his own among his workers on The Grove, but no one had apparently heard or seen anything unusual, and the identity of the culprit remained a mystery.

It was unsettling, but, just as before, several weeks went by with nothing untoward happening, and during that time Frances saw Byron only once when she was in town buying supplies. He did not stop to speak, he merely acknowledged her greeting with a curt nod in passing, and for some unaccountable reason his distant behaviour left her feeling vaguely depressed, but she succeeded later in shrugging it off.

It was during April, three months after she had bought the farm, that her father arrived at Thorndale one morning with a Mr Nel from Phalaborwa. He was interested in buying a herd of forty Afrikaner cattle, consisting of heifers and a few young bulls, but he was so impressed with the cattle Frances had to sell, and the price she quoted, that he eventually bought sixty.

'I brought two trucks with me, Miss King, and I'm afraid I can transport no more than forty cattle to my farm in Phalaborwa,' explained Mr Nel when he had filled in the cheque, and had handed it over to Frances. 'Would it be at all possible for you to deliver the remainder of the cattle to my farm at Phalaborwa?'

Frances considered this for a moment. 'I could deliver them for you, Mr Nel, but I'm afraid it won't be before next week.'

'That would be perfect,' he agreed.

His trucks arrived at Thorndale that same afternoon, and the cattle were loaded on to them in preparation for their long trip to Phalaborwa.

Two days later Frances was called to the stables after dinner to deal with a crisis she had never encountered before. The mare, Princess, had been in labour for some hours, but it seemed as if she was incapable of giving birth to her foal. Frances tried to contact the vet, but she was told that he was out of town for the night and would not be back until the following day. Her next call was to

Mountain View, but Olivia informed her that her father had gone to a farmers' meeting in town, and Frances bit her lip nervously when she replaced the receiver. What was she going to do now?

'Byron will know what to do,' Megan suggested helpfully. 'Why don't you give him a call?'

'No!' Frances snapped at her cousin, shrinking inwardly at the thought of seeking the assistance of a man whom she had begun to think of as her enemy.

'But he's had experience in this sort of thing,' her cousin argued with her.

'I'll manage, thank you,' Frances insisted stubbornly.

'Oh, don't be silly, Frances!' Megan admonished her, reaching for the telephone. 'If you won't ask him to come and help you, then I most certainly will!'

'Byron Rockford is the very last person on earth I would want to approach for help, and you know that!' Frances argued heatedly, turning on her heel and striding out of the house.

It was a dark night, but she was beginning to know her way about the farm as if she had been born there, and she walked at a brisk pace towards the stable where the mare lay alone and in obvious agony. She kneeled down on the hay, disregarding the fact that she was wearing a clean pair of white slacks, and gently stroked the quivering mare's neck.

'I wish I could help you, Princess,' she murmured soothingly, 'but I'm afraid I don't know what to do.'

Princess raised her head with the distinctive white star on the forehead, and whinnied softly as if she understood. Tears filled Frances' eyes, but she dashed them away impatiently with the back of her hand. To sit there and weep was not going to help the mare at all. She had to do something! But what?

She had no idea how much time had elapsed while she had been kneeling there beside the mare, but the sound of a heavy step at the entrance to the stable made her glance over her shoulder to see Byron's khaki-clad frame dwarfing the stable door. That aura of authority was undeniable while he took in the situation at a glance, and her pulse quickened with relief, but she would rather die than let him know how glad she was to see him at that precise moment.

'What do you want?' she demanded coldly, lowering her gaze to her hands, which were stroking the mare's neck gently as if to convey to her in silence that assistance was close at hand.

'I'm here to help you,' he said calmly, kneeling down beside her and running his large hands lightly over the mare's bulging stomach.

'I didn't ask for your help,' she argued despite the fact that she was desperate for any assistance he could give her.

'Megan asked me to come over and lend a hand,' came the harsh reply, 'and in this instance she has more sense than you have.'

Frances did not prolong the argument. She knew she dared not. The mare's life was at stake and, much as she disliked the idea, Byron was the only one available who could help her.

Casting aside her personal feelings, she asked anxiously, 'What do you think is wrong?'

'I'll have to do an internal examination before I can answer that question.' Byron's voice was clipped, his manner knowledgeably authoritative, and in this instance it inspired Frances with confidence rather than anger. 'I suggest you get a bucket of hot water, and soap,' he instructed her. 'A couple of old towels would also come in handy, and I suggest you be quick about it.'

She did not hesitate. She ran all the way through the darkness to the house, and returned a few minutes later with everything he had asked for.

Byron took off his bush jacket, and she could feel her heart beating somewhere in her throat as she watched the powerful play of muscles across his broad back while he washed his arms to well above his elbows.

'I think you'd better talk to her, Frances,' Byron instructed, his hands raised so as not to touch anything when he kneeled down at the mare's rear to proceed with the examination. 'Keep her as calm as you possibly can, because this may take some time.'

Frances yielded to his superior knowledge, and did as she was told, but her heart was thudding nervously and anxiously against her ribs while she watched Byron slide his arm almost elbow-deep into the mare. The glossy brown coat quivered, and Princess raised her head slightly, her eyes rolling nervously and her nostrils flaring as she whinnied softly.

Frances gently stroked her neck, murmuring soothing words of comfort to which the mare seemed to respond, and a few seconds later Frances heard a soft but sharp exclamation pass Byron's lips.

'What is it?' she demanded, her eyes darkening with anxiety in her pale face.

'I've found the problem,' he announced grimly. 'The foal's neck is twisted, and that's why the birth has been delayed.'

'Could you turn it?' she asked, hardly daring to breathe as her glance met Byron's across the prone body of the mare, and he nodded curtly.

'I'm going to have a damn good try.'

Frances seemed to lose all concept of time. It could have been minutes, but it felt more like hours elapsing while she kneeled there on the hard, hay-strewn floor of the stable, talking soothingly to Princess while Byron worked with surprising gentleness in his attempt to turn the foal's head in the correct position prior to birth. Byron was perspiring freely, strands of hair clinging to his damp forehead, and his muscled torso gleaming in the single light that hung from the beams in the roof. It was a hot night and she could feel her blouse clinging to her own damp body, and for the first time in her life a shiver raced up her spine when she heard the mournful howl of a jackal in the distance.

'There!' Byron said eventually, his abrupt exclamation making her insides jolt nervously. 'It's done,' he added with satisfaction.

'She's very weak,' murmured Frances, her glance following Byron anxiously when he got up to wash his arms. 'Do you think she'll be all right?'

'She ought to be,' he said, rinsing the soap off his arms and drying them on a towel before he resumed his kneeling position beside the mare to slide an experienced hand lightly over the mare's belly. 'Come on, Princess,' he urged in a low voice which was almost a growl. 'How about a nice strong contraction, and you'll have your foal in no time.'

Princess obliged him several minutes later, and not long afterwards the foal was born, a colt that looked suspiciously as if it had Arab blood in it. Frances' relief was so intense that she almost cried, but she swallowed down her tears for fear that Byron might notice her weakness and mock her for it.

They used the old towels, rubbing the colt down firmly to stimulate it as the mare would have done if she had not been so weak, and working alongside Byron like that, laughing with him at the almost comical weakness of the foal, made her see him in a totally different light from the one which she had become accustomed to.

'Come on, you little beauty,' she whispered encouragingly, hovering somewhere between laughter and unashamed tears. 'You're weak like your mother, but you're going to be all right.'

It took some time before they managed to get the mare on her feet, and the colt was so wobbly on his legs that they had to guide him towards his mother to drink. They sat on the floor, laughing a little as they slumped back against the wall while they watched the colt drinking, and Frances found herself admitting that her feelings towards Byron had become tempered with admiration and respect. It was getting late, it was almost ten o'clock, but Byron did not leave until both he and Frances were sure that the mare and her foal were out of danger.

Byron shrugged himself into his khaki bush-jacket, but he left it unbuttoned when he accompanied Frances along the path that led to the house. Neither of them spoke, they were both tired, but Frances could feel her mind whirling in a vain attempt to find the appropriate words with which to thank him. There was no sense in denying that, without his valued assistance, the mare might have died.

They were entering the house through the kitchen door, and she was still at a loss for the right words when she turned to him and said simply, 'Thank you, Byron.'

'Don't thank me, Frances,' he smiled down at her with that hint of mockery back in his tawny eyes. 'If it takes a crisis like this to get you to use my name, then you're welcome to my assistance any time you wish.'

Frances coloured slightly and looked away. She had used his name without thinking, it had slipped out so naturally after what they had been through together, but now she felt curiously embarrassed about it.

Megan chose that moment to walk into the kitchen, and she mercifully drew Byron's attention away from Frances.

'I didn't want to intrude in the stables and perhaps get in the way,' she explained her absence unnecessarily, her glance darting anxiously from one to the other. 'Is everything okay?'

'Yes,' Frances answered her, and a look of relief replaced the anxiety in Megan's blue eyes. 'Thanks to Byron,' she added, 'Princess finally succeeded in giving birth to a lovely colt.'

'I wouldn't be surprised if there's a bit of Arab blood in it somewhere,' Byron laughingly echoed Frances' own speculations about the colt's heritage.

'I telephoned your mother earlier this evening,' Megan changed the subject. 'I told her not to worry, and that Byron was here to help you.'

'Thank you, Megan,' Frances smiled tiredly at her cousin. 'That was kind of you.'

'Well, I'm off to bed,' Megan announced, stifling a yawn behind her fingers. 'See you both in the morning.'

Frances was on edge after Megan's hasty departure from the kitchen. She had spent the best part of the evening alone with Byron, but now she was suddenly aware of him as a man, and aware, too, of a frantic fluttering in her breast at the sight of his powerful chest with the dark hair curling tightly against his tanned skin. She had never before met a man whose masculinity was as potent as Byron's, and she felt a vague sense of alarm at the way it appeared to affect her senses.

'I know it's late, but . . .' she gestured expressively with her hands, 'could I offer you a cup of coffee before you leave?'

'I wouldn't say no to that,' he smiled faintly, pulling out a chair and seating himself at the scrubbed wooden table.

Frances turned away from him to switch on the electric kettle, and she was surprised to discover that her hands were trembling visibly. She knew that Byron was watching her while she set out the cups and spooned instant coffee into them, and she could only pray that he would not notice how ridiculously nervous and shy she suddenly felt in his company. Being nervous and shy were two characterisics quite foreign to her nature, but for some diabolical reason she was remembering the way he had kissed her that night at Megan's birthday party, and she was also remembering the way he had made her feel.

You may be a cattle rancher, but you're a woman first, and next time you want to pick a fight, I suggest you choose someone who isn't afraid to cross swords with you!

She doubted if she would ever forget those words he had flung at her so harshly that night after he had kissed her, and she admitted to herself for the first time that she had deserved them. She also had to admit that Byron was a powerful adversary, and that was something she admired in a man.

Dear heaven! What was she thinking?

She placed their cups of coffee on the table and passed Byron the milk and the sugar and, unfortunately, the slight tremor in her hands did not go unnoticed. His tawny gaze sharpened, making her cheeks flare, and it took a moment to regain her composure.

'Byron . . .' she began, breaking the awkward silence between them, and determined to make her peace with him somehow, 'I'm not guilty of cutting the fence, and I believe I can say the same for every one of my workers. They've all lived and worked on this farm for a number of years, and there's absolutely no reason for any one of them to do such a damnable thing.'

He did not answer her at first, and she was beginning to think he had not heard a word she had said when he raised an amused eyebrow and smiled twistedly. 'I believe you,' he said unexpectedly, 'and I owe you an apology for my unjust accusations the first time it happened.'

'Your apology is accepted,' she returned his smile ruefully, 'but it doesn't exactly solve the problem, does it? We still don't know who the culprit is.'

'That may take a little time,' he agreed, frowning down into his coffee, then he changed the subject. 'Megan tells me you're taking a truckload of cattle through to Phalaborwa next week.'

'Yes,' she confirmed, wondering why her trip to Phalaborwa should interest him. 'I'm leaving here late Tuesday afternoon, and I'm going to do most of the travelling after dark when it's cool.'

'I wonder if you would do me a favour?' he said, studying her contemplatively. 'I can get three lions, a male and two females, from a chap who owns a game park a few kilometres outside Phalaborwa. If I could arrange with him to prepare the lions for transportation, do you think you could bring them back to Izilwane on your truck?'

Frances realised charitably that one favour deserved another. Her truck was, after all, returning empty . . . but lions? She felt a shudder rippling through her when she met his steady, questioning glance.

'I presume they'll be in crates?' she asked cautiously.

There was a gleam of mockery in the tawny gaze that held hers. 'They'll be in crates used for transporting animals, and it ought to be quite safe.'

She noted nervously that he had said it *ought to be quite safe*. How safe, exactly, would it be, or was she looking for problems where none existed?

'If they're going to be in crates, then I'll transport them for you,' she finally agreed, but the thought of lion in the game park sent an unexpected chill racing through her. They had enough problems with some crazy person tearing down the fence between their properties, and animals wandering through. But what if the fence was cut again and this time a lion got through to her cattle?

'Are you going to drive the truck yourself?' Byron questioned her, interrupting her frightening thoughts while they were drinking their coffee, and she shook her head.

'Sipho will be driving the truck, and I'm going with him to make sure that nothing goes wrong with the delivery.'

'I have a better idea.' He drained his cup and pushed it aside to rest his arms on the table. 'Leave Sipho here to keep an eye on the farm. You and I could do the trip together in the truck, and I'll act as your driver.'

'That sounds like a good idea,' she admitted.

She had been rather worried about leaving the farm with only the herdsmen in attendance, but, when she thought of the long hours she would have to spend alone with Byron in the truck, she was not so sure if it was a good idea at all. It was much too late now to do anything about it. Byron would know that she was nervous of being alone with him if she suddenly changed her mind, and his mockery was something she could do without.

Byron left a few minutes later, promising to let her know when his arrangements were finalised, and Frances took Major with her for a walk to the stables for another quick look at the mare and her foal before she went to bed.

CHAPTER SIX

A DANCE, with dinner included, was held at Izilwane on the Saturday evening. Tony persuaded Frances to accompany him, and Megan went with Jack Harriman, one of the game wardens. A three-piece band from Louisville provided the music, and the thatch-roofed restaurant with its log-cabin décor was filled to capacity with locals and visitors on holiday in the game park. It was a casual affair, the food was excellent, and Megan and her tanned, sandy-haired friend were pleasant company.

For the second time within a few short months Frances had cause to set foot on Izilwane soil. She had, at first, been on edge at the thought of meeting Byron, but he did not put in an appearance, and as the evening wore on she began to relax and enjoy herself.

She had danced several times with Tony, but when the band lapsed into a wild disco beat he steered her towards the glass doors leading out of the restaurant. The night air was cool and refreshing, and her arm was linked casually through his as they strolled towards the pool area, which was deserted at that time of the night. The music coming from the restaurant was muted, but it was still loud enough to drown out the night sounds of the bushveld, and Frances drew the fresh, scented air deep into her lungs.

'Have you given any thought to our relationship lately?' Tony broke the companionable silence between them, his lean, handsome features strangely rigid in the moonlight.

'In what way do you mean?' she asked warily.

'We've been seeing quite a lot of each other since we became neighbours, and during the past three months we've got to know each other quite well, wouldn't you say?'

'Yes, that's true,' she admitted, wondering what this odd conversation was leading up to.

'I would say we know each other well enough, in fact, to start thinking of marriage.'

'*Marriage?*' Frances echoed, startled into immobility, and she removed her arm from his as if his touch had stung her.

What was the matter with Tony? Their relationship had been comfortable and friendly. There had never been anything physical between them, she had made it quite clear from the start that she had no desire for the casual kisses and the petting which usually occurred in a relationship between a man and a woman, and she had most certainly done nothing to give him reason to believe that she would agree to a deeper, more intimate relationship with him.

'Think of the possibilities which could arise,' Tony continued excitedly, seemingly quite oblivious of the fact that she was staring at him as if he had suddenly become deranged. 'The Grove and Thorndale could become one farm, and together we could make it the most successful farm in the district. Just think of that, Frances, and just think about how we could——'

'Wait a minute, Tony!' she interrupted him firmly, raising her hands in a silencing gesture which he could not ignore. 'I like you, and I appreciate your friendship, but that's all there will ever be between us.'

'You don't mean that,' he laughed, and in the moonlight his handsome features were etched in disbelief as if a woman's rejection was something he had never encountered before.

'I'm afraid I do mean it,' she was forced to disillusion him cruelly. 'I'm sorry.'

'But you like me, you said so yourself, and if you'd only give yourself a chance, you could learn to love me!' There was a hint of anxiety in his eyes which she could not understand as he reached for her. 'I'll prove it to you!'

There was something desperate and unfamiliar about him when he caught her round the waist and pulled her towards him. She did not like the feel of his body against her own and, when he made an attempt to kiss her, she turned her face away so that his hot, moist mouth brushed against her jaw close to her ear.

'Don't be silly, Tony!' she rebuked him sharply, suppressing a shiver of revulsion as she placed her hands flat against his chest and pushed him away from her with every ounce of strength she possessed. 'Stop that!'

His arms fell limply at his sides, and he was breathing heavily as he stood facing her. 'What's the matter with you, Frances?'

'I could ask you the same question,' she accused bluntly. 'You're behaving irrationally, and you'll spoil our friendship if you don't pull yourself together.'

A look of anger flashed across his face, but it was gone the next instant. 'I'm sorry, but I thought——' He shrugged off the rest of his sentence, and gestured towards the restaurant where the the dance was still in progress. 'Shall we go inside?'

'You go, Tony,' she suggested, needing time to overcome the shock of what had occurred. 'I'd really like to be alone for a while.'

'Very well,' he agreed amiably, eager to make amends as if he realised suddenly that he had overstepped the mark. 'But don't be too long,' he added, flashing his familiar smile.

She watched him walk away, then she subsided into a chair beside the pool and stared at the silvery, motionless sheet of water. She wondered again about Tony. He had behaved rather strangely, and she was still baffled by his unexpected and odd proposal of marriage when she heard a step behind her on the tiled edge of the pool.

Frances rose abruptly, thinking it was Tony, but she turned to find Byron's tall, bulky frame confronting her, and her angry retort died on her lips. She had not thought that she would ever have cause to feel relieved to see Byron, but at that moment she was experiencing such a sensation, and perhaps that was why the first words he uttered had the strange power to hurt as well as annoy her.

'Was that a lovers' quarrel I witnessed a few moments ago?' he questioned her with that hateful hint of mockery in his deep, gravelly voice, and her body stiffened with resentment.

'That's none of your business!' she snapped, taking in his familiar khaki pants and bush-jacket, and aware of his eyes roaming over her taut body with the wide skirt of her floral silk dress stirring about her legs in the gentle breeze.

'He's not the right man for you, Frances,' Byron announced with infuriating arrogance.

'You're not in a position to judge who is, or who isn't, the right man for me,' she answered him coldly, turning to walk away from him, but fingers of steel closed like a vice about her arm to prevent her from leaving.

'Come with me,' he instructed, striding away from the pool, and taking her along with him despite her efforts to free herself from his clasp.

'No!' she protested hotly. 'Let me go!'

'I want to show you something which you ought to see on a night like this when the moon is full,' he explained without halting his long strides, and Frances, despite the length of her own legs, found that she virtually had to run to keep up with him.

'Tony will wonder what has happened to me, and so will Megan,' she persisted frantically when she realised he was taking her to where he had parked his Land Rover along the side of his bungalow, and she saw Byron's rugged features crease in a mocking smile.

'I sent a message to Megan to let her know you're with me, but Tony can wonder as much as he pleases.'

'You had no right to do such a thing without first consulting me!' she stormed at him, almost choking on

the words in her anger, and shrinking away physically
when he opened the Land Rover door on the passenger
side. 'Byron, I'm not going anywhere with you.'

'Get in, we're wasting time,' he said tersely, eyeing her
speculatively. 'Or do I have to pick you up and put you
in?'

There was no way she could escape him, she knew
that, and the thought of him picking her up and putting
her into the Land Rover was too humiliating to
contemplate. She glared up at him furiously, but she got
into the Land Rover without further arguments, and sat
there stiffly while he walked round the bonnet to get in
behind the wheel.

'Where are you taking me?' she demanded a few
minutes later, when they had left the enclosure of the
camp and were driving slowly along one of the tracks
through the game park.

'You'll find out soon enough,' he said abruptly,
concentrating on his driving and keeping a sharp lookout
for animals which might have strayed into the road.

Some minutes later Frances caught a brief glimpse of a
large expanse of water shimmering in the moonlight, and
she began to suspect what Byron had in mind long before
he parked his Land Rover beside the dam at the entrance
to the narrow wooden pier where the motor launch was
moored.

He opened the door for her to get out, but she jerked
her arm free of his clasp when he attempted to usher her
towards the pier. 'I'm not going on that launch with you.'

'Oh, yes, you are!'

He turned towards her as he spoke and, before she
could guess his intentions, his arms were like steel bands
about her waist and behind her knees. It had all
happened so quickly, and so unexpectedly, that her arms
circled his neck in an instinctive need for support when
she was lifted off her feet, and he was striding along the
pier with her as if she weighed nothing at all, his
footsteps heavy on the wooden planks.

'Put me down, Byron!' she protested furiously, the flags of humiliation in her cheeks mercifully not visible in the moonlight as she tried desperately to free herself.

'If you don't stop struggling we could both end up in the water, and I don't fancy myself as a meal for the crocodiles,' Byron warned harshly.

Crocodiles? Frances stilled in his arms. She had no desire to feed herself to the crocodiles, but Byron was an equally dangerous element, and finding herself trapped between the two was not a situation she was relishing.

He carried her towards the end of the pier and on to the launch, and did not put her down until he stood in front of the controls.

'Are there crocodiles in this dam?' she asked, a whisper of doubt entering her mind as she stared at his rugged but attractive profile against the night sky when the engines came throbbingly alive beneath his hands.

'No,' he smiled at her mockingly, and it took a stunned moment for her to realise that she had been duped.

'You *beast*!' she cried, turning on him in a blind fury to beat at his chest and shoulders with her clenched fists. 'You lied to me! You *lied*!'

Strong fingers gripped her wrists, and her arms were twisted behind her back to be held there with one large hand while the other grasped a handful of her long dark hair to jerk her head back. She was trapped against his bulky frame, her breasts hurting against his hard chest, and her scalp smarting. She made a desperate attempt to free herself, but every writhing movement intensified her awareness of the hard male body against her own, and she stilled her efforts abruptly to glare up into eyes which were observing her with tolerant amusement.

'Damn you, Byron, let me go!' she hurled at him in a furious, helpless rage.

'In my own good time, you shrew,' he growled, lowering his head and trailing his warm mouth along the column of her exposed throat with shattering results.

With the ease of a man who had an intimate

knowledge of women, Byron found those sensitive areas
which she had not known existed, and a thousand little
nerves suddenly came alive beneath the coaxing exploration of his sensuous mouth to send shafts of unwanted
pleasure darting through her.

What was he doing to her? What was this pulsating
warmth which was flowing through her body until her
taut muscles relaxed and she melted against him? No!
She did not want him to do this to her! her confused mind
shrieked, but she could not control the feelings storming
through her to take possession of her body.

Her heart was beating hard and fast against her ribs as
if it was competing with the throbbing engines of the
stationary launch, and the moon seemed to dip and sway
in the star-studded sky before her eyelids fluttered down
as if they had become weighted with lead. The quivering
of her lips was stilled a moment later when Byron's
mouth shifted over hers, demanding a response from her
which she was incapable of withholding and, her hands
released, she clung to his wide shoulders, aware of the
play of muscles through the cloth of his bush-jacket as
she felt herself drowning in the swamp of her own
emotions.

Byron's hands slowly roamed her pliant body, sliding
over the gentle curve of her hips, and moving upwards
again to cup her firm breasts through the silk of her dress.
She ought to have rejected this intimate exploration, but
her mind was no longer in control as her body responded
with a knowledge of its own, and her nipples hardened
beneath the caress of his thumbs, awakening her to an
aching stab of desire that made her utter a sound like a
whimper against Byron's mouth.

She was dazed and trembling when he finally released
her. She was also confused and bewildered as she stared
up into his shadowy face in the hope of finding the
answer there.

'That was something of a revelation, wasn't it?' he
announced, the mockery in his voice stabbing painfully

deep. 'Don't tell me I've succeeded in rendering you speechless for once?'

'You're contemptible!' she hissed, shame and fury mingling with a force that brought tears to her eyes, and she turned hastily, aware of an intense desire to flee, but in some uncanny way Byron had latched on to her thoughts.

He opened the throttle to full power, and the launch pulled away from the pier with a violent lurch that sent her staggering into one of the seats to sit there, fuming inwardly and blind for some time to the beauty surrounding her.

Byron steered the launch towards the centre of the dam and, her anger abating, Frances found her attention captured by the moonlit landscape spread out all around her. She got up to stand beside the rail, and she could not help thinking that it looked as if the stars had descended from the velvety darkness of the sky to dance on the ripples of the water.

The engines ceased their rhythmic throbbing, and during the ensuing silence Frances felt her aggression desert her to leave her strangely at peace. The water lapped gently against the side of the stationary launch, and somewhere in the game park a jackal howled, the sound drifting clearly across the water towards her. The veld was lit with a silvery glow, and it deepened the shadows mysteriously beneath the bushes and the trees. Frances felt as if she had been given a glimpse of paradise, and she was convinced that God had dipped his artistic brush in the full moon that night to add a brilliant touch of magic to the scenario.

'Isn't this worth seeing?' Byron asked with a smile in his voice when he joined her at the rail.

'Yes, it is,' she agreed with a near ecstatic sigh, and her anger of a few minutes ago was forgotten.

'When I was a small boy I used to dream of having a place like Izilwane,' he told her something about himself which she felt sure not many people knew.

It was not difficult to believe that he had nurtured his dream for so many years, but she had difficulty in trying to imagine him as a small boy.

'You're fortunate that your dream became a reality,' she said, capturing a strand of hair which the breeze had lifted across her face, and securing it behind her ear.

'What did you dream of when you were a little girl, Frances?' he asked, leaning against the rail and turning his head to look at her with a faint smile playing about his sensuous mouth as if he, too, was having difficulty in trying to imagine her as a child.

'I dreamed of being a cattle rancher like my father.' A reminiscent smile curved her lips. 'He didn't like the idea at first, but I had Olivia on my side, and my father eventually relented.'

'I've gathered that Olivia is not your own mother.'

'No, she isn't,' Frances confirmed. 'My mother died when I was four, and my father married Olivia when I was ten.'

'Were you unhappy about that?' asked Byron, studying her intently as if to gauge her feelings.

'Not at all,' she shook her head adamantly, and her smile deepened. 'Olivia is a warm, generous, and adorable woman, and I can remember wishing with all my heart that she would marry my father.' She glanced at Byron questioningly. 'Tell me about your parents?'

'They died when I was a child, and I grew up in the home of an aunt who had never married,' he explained without a trace of emotion in his deep voice. 'I was pleasantly surprised when she died some years ago and left me a small fortune. I had worked hard and, by choice, I often had to survive on the bare necessities, but in that way I'd accumulated a small fortune of my own, and that was how I managed to buy this piece of ground for the game park.'

Frances felt a stab of compassion mingling with her growing admiration. 'I don't suppose you've ever regretted your decision?'

'Never.' His eyes glittered with that familiar mockery when they met hers. 'Have you?'

'No, never,' she responded without hesitation, 'and meeting an arrogant and conceited man like you has only made me more determined to succeed.'

Byron laughed softly. 'If I seem arrogant and conceited, then I apologise, but I'm still of the opinion that farming isn't a woman's job.'

'And I'm still equally determined to prove you wrong.'

'You don't have to prove anything to me, Frances,' he brushed aside her defiant statement. 'It's yourself you have to convince that you made the right decision in the choice of your career.'

'I don't need convincing. I know I made the right decision.'

'Then my arrogant and conceited opinion shouldn't matter to you,' he pointed out with a bluntness that stung.

His opinion shouldn't matter to her, but in some strange way it did. Why?

'Take one good look around you, Frances,' he interrupted her bewildered thoughts, 'and if you can appreciate what you see, then you must realise that I was right in saying that Tony isn't the man for you.'

'Don't tell me you're concerned for my sake?' she responded without anger, but with a hint of mockery in her soft laughter when she discovered the reason for this moonlight excursion on the launch.

'Strange as it may seem, I am concerned,' he said with an odd gravity in his deep voice. 'You have a genuine love of the land, Frances, and I'm not blind to the fact that you're not afraid to work hard at what you're doing, but Tony Phillips is not interested in what he can put into the land. To him it's what he can get out of it that matters.'

That was true. It had not taken her long to discover that Tony was an uninterested rancher, but she had no desire to discuss Tony or their friendship with Byron.

'I'll keep that in mind,' she promised soberly.

The breeze darted playfully through her long hair, which she had left free of confinement that evening, and this time it was Byron who lifted a strand away from her face to tuck it behind her ear. He did not remove his hand, and the faint smell of his masculine cologne stirred her senses when he trailed an exploratory finger across her cheekbone and down along the side of her jaw.

His touch was disturbing, and there was an extraordinary tension in the atmosphere between them that made her pulse quicken when she looked up into his rugged face, and her glance lingered on that dark curl which threatened to spill on to his broad forehead.

He lowered his head as she raised hers. It was an act which was conducted simultaneously, as if something far beyond their control had taken charge of their actions, and a quivering warmth erupted deep inside her when their lips met, lightly at first, and then with a deeper need that drove her into strong arms which were ready to receive her.

She did not pause to question what was happening to her. She knew the truth as if it was something she had known all her life, but the truth was accompanied by an unfamiliar fear and uncertainty that made her withdraw from him mentally as well as physically to stand trembling in the wake of her discovery.

She was in love with Byron, but, for her own peace of mind, she must never let him guess it.

'Please take me back, Byron,' she said huskily, staring out across the shimmering water to avoid the query in his probing eyes, and her heart leapt nervously into her throat when she felt him hesitate beside her, but she need not have been afraid.

Byron walked away from her towards the controls, and a moment later the rhythmic throbbing of the engines disturbed the silence of that incredibly beautiful night.

Frances remained standing at the rail while the launch chugged back to its moorings, and it was fear of exposing her feelings that made her ignore his helping hand on to the pier. They did not speak to each other during the drive back to the camp, but it was Byron who broke the strained silence between them when he had parked his Land Rover along the side of his bungalow.

'Everything is arranged,' he said. 'We may collect the lions at Phalaborwa next Wednesday.'

Byron's voice had been cold and clipped like that of a stranger, convincing her that he had been left emotionally untouched by what had happened between them on the launch, and she nodded in reply to his statement as she got out of the Land Rover, her throat suddenly too tight to speak.

She walked away from him along the flagstone path leading towards the restaurant, and she was grateful that she had these few moments alone before she joined the others. She had to accept what had happened to her, and she had to come to terms with it. Byron did not care for her, and he never would. The only thing he cared about was Izilwane, his dream, and what had occurred between them could be labelled as nothing more than a mild flirtation. She had to remember that his masculine virility was not a pose, and they had been alone on that launch in a setting which might have turned any man's head.

Frances entered the crowded restaurant, her sensitive ears protesting at the blaring loudness of the music, and she saw Tony rising agitatedly from his chair when she approached their table.

'Where the hell have you been?' he demanded angrily.

'I was . . .' She caught a warning look in Megan's blue eyes, and decided against relating the truth to Tony. 'I went for a long walk.'

'It must have been one hell of a long walk,' he responded churlishly, but he studied her speculatively once they were seated. 'Were you alone?'

His attitude was beginning to annoy her, and it was also making Jack Harriman and Megan shift about uncomfortably in their chairs, but she forced a smile to her lips. 'Stop being silly, Tony, and stop this unnecessary cross-examination.'

'I need to go to the ladies' room,' Megan intervened, rising from her chair before Tony could respond to Frances' remark. 'Are you coming with me, Frances?'

'Yes,' Frances answered abruptly, picking up her evening bag as she rose from her chair, and following Megan from the restaurant and across the foyer of the building to the ladies' room.

'Where in heaven's name *have* you been all this time?' Megan confronted her laughingly the moment they were alone. 'Do you realise you were gone for almost an hour?'

'Byron took me on to the dam in the launch.'

'Oh, did he?' Megan smiled faintly, and Frances could guess what was going on in her cousin's mind. 'We talked,' she explained bluntly, and Megan nodded with a knowing look in her eyes.

'A romantic setting is always the best place to be when a man and a woman need to talk.'

'Oh, Megan!' Frances laughed away her cousin's remark, but she was crying inside.

She had always believed that it would be a momentous and happy occasion when she discovered that she was in love, but she had never dreamed it would be with a man who had gone out of his way from the start to make her dislike him intensely, and whom she still thought of as arrogant, conceited, and condescending.

Why, oh, why did fate have to be so cruel?

Taking the truckload of cattle to a farm in the Phalaborwa district was not something which Frances had been looking forward to and, to make matters worse, the atmosphere was incredibly strained between Byron and herself when they left Thorndale late on the Tuesday afternoon of the following week. Frances knew that she was partly to blame for the chilly situation between them. She was so afraid that she might say or do something to make Byron realise how she felt about him that she had been rudely abrupt with him at the start of the journey, and his equally abrupt response had resulted in the stony silence which dominated the atmosphere in the cab of the truck for more than an hour.

Frances also had something else on her mind. She did not like the idea of Byron introducing lion into the game park while the culprit who had cut the fence between their properties was still at large. A recurrence of that offence, with lions roaming free, made her shudder inwardly.

Byron pulled the truck off the road at dusk, and they got out to stretch their legs and check on the cattle before she poured coffee from the flask she had packed. She passed Byron a mug, and his tawny eyes smiled at her when he raised it to his lips. It was a mocking but strangely infectious smile, and she could not prevent herself from responding to it.

'I'm sorry I snapped at you when you arrived at the farm this afternoon,' she felt compelled to apologise, and his tawny gaze roamed over her tall, slender, denim-clad figure leaning against the dusty truck.

'You've obviously got something on your mind that's bothering you.' He studied her intently while he sipped his hot coffee. 'Would you like to talk about it?'

She had several things on her mind that were bothering her, but the only one she dared discuss with him was the reason for his presence on this trip to Phalaborwa with her.

'I don't like the thought of your lions getting through on to my property,' she explained, and his dark brows drew together in an angry frown.

'You're being unnecessarily pessimistic, Frances.'

'It's all very well for you to say that,' she argued, 'but what if the fence is cut again and some of my cattle are killed, or my herdsmen are attacked by one of your lions?'

'You will naturally be adequately compensated for the loss of your cattle, but if your herdsmen are attacked, then our mysterious offender will have a hell of a lot more to answer for.'

Frances felt little shivers racing along her spine while they drank their coffee and returned their empty mugs to the basket. She was not prone to premonitions, but she was labouring under a distinctly uneasy feeling, and she had no idea what it was. She was also afraid. She had never before had reason to be afraid of anything, and she did not quite know how to cope with it.

'You have nothing to be afraid of,' Byron said as if he had read her thoughts. 'The chances are very slim that one of my lions will get through on to your property. They won't be looking for a way out of the game park where there's enough place to roam, and enough food, so don't anticipate the worst.'

'I guess you think I'm being silly,' she laughed, but there was no humour in the sound of her laughter.

'Not silly,' he contradicted, lessening the distance between them in one long stride to tip her face up to his with his fingers beneath her chin. 'Just wary in the same way I am.'

The smell of the sun and the bush clung to his khaki clothes, and she found that she had to contend with the unexpected desire to lean against his hard male body. She was also intensely aware of her weakness as a woman, and the need to feel the comforting strength of his arms about her.

She had to pull herself together, she told herself, but Byron seemed to sense her need in the same uncanny way he had succeeded in reading her thoughts a few moments ago, and he lowered his head to kiss her lightly on the lips before he drew her into his arms. He held her with her head resting comfortably against the hollow of his shoulder, and a tired little sigh escaped her as she slipped her arms about his lean waist.

Why fight it and deny it? she asked herself. She was encountering a strange new peace in Byron's arms, and it flowed like a warm tide through her. She might regret it later. She might regret showing him that underneath her determined, often tough, exterior she was still a woman with a woman's weaknesses, but at that moment she could only think that it felt so right to be standing there in the circle of his arms with her head resting on his shoulder where she could hear the strong, heavy beat of his heart.

'It's time to move on,' he said eventually, releasing her, and his face wore an unperturbed, expressionless mask when she stood facing him in the gathering dusk.

It had meant nothing to him. The brief closeness they had shared had left him untouched. Oh, God, what a fool she was to reach out for something which could never be hers but for a fleeting moment!

CHAPTER SEVEN

FRANCES blinked in the darkness just before dawn, and drew the cool, crisp air into her lungs on a jerky, nervous breath as she watched the crates with their savage contents being loaded on to her truck. A small group of men, shirtless and in shorts, were heaving and pushing, their faces showing visible signs of strain, and their back and arm muscles bulging in the headlights of the two stationary jeeps which illuminated the area.

She was looking at Byron, in particular, working as part of the team. A dark brown curl clung to his damp forehead, and his strong teeth flashed in a smile at a remark passed by one of the men. They had spent the night in the home of Petrus Nel and his wife, the rancher to whom she had delivered the cattle, but Frances had slept badly. She had had a recurring nightmare and, standing there outside the arc of the headlights, she wondered if she was awake, or if this was merely an extension of her nightmare.

The third and last crate had to be lifted on to the truck. The lioness with the torn ear was obviously a fighter, and the most savage of the three lions. Her claws were extended, and she lashed out repeatedly through the bars of the crate at anyone who ventured too close. Her yellow eyes glowed with a fierce fire, her lips drawn back to expose deadly fangs which could tear effortlessly into the flesh of her prey, and Frances felt herself quivering like an animal which had detected the smell of a lion on the hunt.

Byron was inserting a dart into a rifle, his rugged features calm, and a faint smile about his mouth as if he found the lioness's savage temperament amusing. Dear God, did nothing ever frighten him? He raised the rifle,

taking aim with the butt steadied against his shoulder,
and Frances swallowed convulsively when she saw his
finger curl about the trigger. For the third time that
morning there was a loud crack, but this time it made her
nerves jolt, and the proud beast grunted, a startled
expression entering those yellow eyes before they became
glazed with the effect of the drug. The tawny body sagged
slowly on to the floor of the crate, and suddenly she
looked like a harmless kitten instead of a vicious jungle
cat.

Frances was still shaking half an hour later when she
was sitting beside Byron in the cab of the truck at the
start of their four-hour journey back to Louisville, but it
was fortunately too dark for him to notice anything
unusual about her.

'You're very quiet,' he said eventually when the
greyness of dawn was stealing across the sky.

What did she say to that? She could conjure up an
acceptable excuse for her unnatural behaviour, but her
inherent honesty would not allow an evasion of that
nature.

'I've never been this close to a lion before, and
knowing that there are three of them on the truck is
unnerving,' she confessed, staring straight ahead at the
road winding its way among the timber forests and fruit
and vegetable plantations.

They were approaching Tzaneen, a beautiful old town
at the centre of a large and varying farming community,
which lay at the foot of the Drakensberg on the south
bank of the Great Letaba River. They still had a long
way to go to get to Louisville, Frances thought, sighing
inwardly as she glanced at the lush scenery surrounding
them.

'I didn't think you frightened easily,' Byron laughed
softly.

'I don't usually, but there's something about the lioness
with the torn ear that makes my blood run cold.' She
clenched her hands in her lap and suppressed a shiver.

'She's older than the other two, and she has an unpredictable temperament.'

Out of the corner of her eye she could see Byron break the concentration of his driving to glance at her briefly. 'Females have a tendency to be temperamental.'

Frances turned to look at him with a hint of anger in her dark eyes. 'Why do I have the feeling you're no longer referring to females of the feline species?'

'You're very much like that big cat,' he insisted with a mocking smile curving his sensuous mouth. 'One minute you're purring like a kitten, and the next you're spitting like a wildcat with your claws unsheathed. You are, in fact, the most temperamental female I've ever met.'

'I'm not like that at all!' Frances protested, feeling vaguely disconcerted, but hiding her reaction behind a cynical smile. 'Perhaps you simply succeed in bringing out the worst in me.

'I wonder why,' he remarked with his own infuriating brand of cynicism.

'It's probably a chemical reaction,' she explained, hiding her growing misery behind a casual demeanour. 'When we're put together we tend to knock sparks off each other.'

'Is that good or bad?' he demanded mockingly.

'I'm not sure,' she confessed, a mirthless smile curving her tight mouth. 'It could be a sign of rejection on both sides.'

Byron appeared to consider this for a moment, then he nodded gravely in agreement. 'You're probably right.'

His answer was as unexpected as the unfamiliar and painful weight that settled in her chest. If this was how it felt to love someone who could never care for you in return, then she would have to do something about conquering her feelings while they were still in their infancy, but something warned her that it was not going to be as easy as she might imagine it would be.

They stopped along the way to drink coffee and to eat the sandwiches Mrs Nel had insisted on making for

them, and somehow kept up a flowing conversation
during the remainder of the trip, but the subject matter
they chose was impersonal, and it seemed to create a
wide chasm between them which neither of them had
any inclination to breach.

Byron dropped Frances off at Thorndale with the
assurance that he would return her truck and collect his
Land Rover as soon as he had off-loaded the lions, which
were now beginning to move about restlessly in their
confining crates. Frances had a final, brief glimpse of the
lioness with the torn ear, and those yellow eyes, staring
back at her unwaveringly, sent a renewed shiver racing
along her spine as she watched the truck disappear along
the avenue of jacaranda trees with Byron at the wheel.

'There's been an interesting development while you
were away,' Megan announced when they were seated at
the luncheon table that day. 'Tony's cousin, Claudia de
Leur, arrived at Izilwane late yesterday afternoon, and
she booked herself into one of the bungalows for an
indefinite period. She's a divorcee from East London in
the Cape Province, and she didn't hesitate to make it
known that she's a niece of the late George Wilkins.'

'Is that so?' Frances murmured without interest,
helping herself to a second cup of tea, and brushing a
stray strand of hair away from her hot face.

'She's also very keen to make the acquaintance of
Thorndale's new owner, meaning you,' Megan added,
her clear blue eyes troubled, 'and I think she's of the
opinion that she should have had a stake in that poor old
man's earthly possessions.'

Frances raised eyes that were showing visible signs of
her nightmare-ridden night, and she sighed heavily. 'I
hope she's not going to involve me in a tiresome battle by
contesting her uncle's will.'

'I certainly hope not,' grimaced Megan, 'but I
understood from the girl at reception that Mrs de Leur
would like to meet you, and that, for old times' sake,
she'd very much like to visit her late uncle's home.'

Frances' glance toured the room, lingering in turn on the blue and gold floral curtains at the window, the carpeted floor, and the beautiful old dining-room table and dresser which had come alive after the wood had been treated and oiled. She could remember how the room had looked before they had cleared it of all its bric-a-brac, and an amused smile curved her mouth.

'There's nothing much left for Claudia de Leur to see except the odd pieces of furniture which were worth keeping,' she murmured her thoughts aloud.

'I told her precisely that when she came to the curio shop this morning, but she insists that she still wants to see the house.' The sound of a car approaching the homestead made Megan rise hastily to look out of the window. 'Speak of the devil,' said Megan, peering through the lace curtain. 'Claudia de Leur is here now, and she's got Byron with her.'

Frances was aware of an obstruction in her throat, and she swallowed down the last mouthful of tea with difficulty before she got up from the table in time to see Byron walking towards the house, shortening his usually long strides to accommodate those of the small, shapely, and extremely attractive blonde who was clinging to his arm as if she wanted to become attached to it permanently.

She felt a stab of something which she was determined to ignore and, wiping her clammy hands down the sides of her denims, she walked out of the dining-room with Megan following close behind her to confront her visitors as they stepped up on to the cool, shaded verandah. Byron's rugged features wore an unfathomable expression, but there was laughter lurking in his eyes as if he had shared a joke of an intimate nature with Claudia de Leur.

'Good afternoon.' Frances' greeting included Byron, but she hastily avoided his tawny glance, and concentrated on the woman who was still clinging possessively to his arm. 'I have been expecting you, Mrs de Leur.'

'Oh, have you?' the blonde smiled sweetly, but her grey eyes were coldly speculative and calculating, and her full, scarlet lips pouted, making Frances feel oddly at a disadvantage with her face devoid of make-up after having spent several hours in the hot sun that morning. 'I hope you don't mind,' Claudia de Leur continued in her seductively husky voice, 'but it's such a long time since my last visit to Thorndale that I asked Byron to accompany me in case I got lost.'

Byron? Frances felt a sharp twinge of displeasure which she was not yet ready to analyse.

'Claudia, I'd like you to meet Frances King, the new owner of Thorndale,' Byron introduced them formally.

Claudia? Frances' eyebrows rose in a faintly sardonic arch above the steady, unwavering gaze of her dark eyes. It had certainly not taken them long to get on to first-name terms with each other, and it was quite apparent that Claudia de Leur was not someone who believed in wasting time where men were concerned. She was obviously not inexperienced in these matters, and neither was Byron. They were two of a kind, Frances decided, and they were welcome to each other.

Aware suddenly of Megan hovering behind her, Frances turned and drew her forward. 'I believe you've met my cousin, Megan O'Brien.'

'Yes, we met this morning in the curio shop,' Claudia de Leur acknowledged Megan with a cool smile and a brief inclination of her blonde head, which Frances was beginning to suspect came out of a bottle.

'Won't you come inside?' Frances invited, conscious of Byron observing her with an amused expression in his eyes which aroused her to an inexplicable anger, but she suppressed it as she led the way across the hall into the lounge.

'My goodness! You have made the place look quite attractive, but making changes like this costs money, and Uncle George was always a mean old devil. He would never have——' Claudia de Leur halted abruptly, her grey eyes wide and startled as she stared at the lifelike portrait of George Wilkins hanging against the wall. 'For God's sake, it's the old devil himself!'

'We found it among some of his possessions, and it's such a good portrait that we didn't have the heart to get rid of it,' Frances explained, for some peculiar reason not going into detail about the exact circumstances of her discovery, but she felt compelled to add, 'since you're one of his two remaining relatives, would you perhaps like to have this portrait of your uncle?'

'No, thank you.' Claudia de Leur's rejection of the portrait was instantaneous and as adamant as Tony's had been, but, unlike Tony, she tried to explain her reason for not wanting it, and she did so rather hastily and in a way which made Frances suspect that dear Uncle George's niece was trying to cover up something. 'I live in a tiny flat at the moment, and I don't have space on my walls for a portrait that size,' she explained.

'Was there anything in particular you wanted to see?' Frances changed the subject.

'Nothing in particular,' Claudia de Leur announced, releasing Byron's arm for the first time with a display of reluctance, 'but I would like to take a walk through the old house, if you don't mind.'

'I'll ask Gladys to make a fresh pot of tea while you take Mrs de Leur on a tour of the house,' Megan intervened for the first time, and Frances nodded her approval before she led the way from the lounge, where Byron chose to remain.

'It certainly brings back fond memories to see this old piece of furniture,' Claudia de Leur announced ten minutes later when they stood beside the desk in Frances' small study.

Scarlet-tipped fingers slid along the carved edges of the desk which had once belonged to George Wilkins, and they did so in much the same manner they had done when she had examined the mirrored dresser in the dining-room. A peculiar sensation rippled through

Frances, alerting her to something, but she could not imagine what it was at that precise moment.

'Did you come here often?' she asked, observing the blonde, elegantly clad woman intently, and wondering what lay behind those grey, calculating eyes which had swept every room in the house with such keen interest.

'As a child I came here quite often with my mother. Uncle George was her brother, you see,' Claudia de Leur smiled, but the smile did not reach her eyes, which were as cold as the diamonds glittering on her fingers in the shaft of sunlight entering the room through the window. 'After my mother died I somehow never found the time to visit him again. You know how it is.'

No, Frances did not know how it was. Her family had always played a very important role in her life. She loved each one of them very dearly, and nothing on earth would have induced her to stay away from any one of them for a period long enough to alienate her from them. The mere thought of such an uncaring attitude was distasteful to her.

'Are you aware that you have a cousin living on a neighbouring farm?' she asked, and a strangely blank look settled on Claudia de Leur's painted face. 'Tony Phillips?' Frances prompted her.

'Yes, I know about Tony,' came the abrupt reply, and Frances found the woman's heady perfume repelling to her sensitive nostrils when Claudia slowly circled the desk a second time. 'I must say I find it incredible to believe that my uncle sold everything the way he did. Was there nothing in his will stating that certain pieces of furniture were to be left to his family?'

'I bought the farm as it stood,' Frances informed her with a measure of distaste. 'I'm not aware of the exact contents of your uncle's will, but if you're seeking information in that respect, I suggest you make an appointment to see your uncle's lawyer, Thomas Atherstone, in Louisville.'

'I think perhaps I'll do that.' Claudia de Leur turned,

and her grey eyes studied Frances with a curious intensity. 'Was the portrait the only thing of interest you found when you went through Uncle George's possessions?'

There was a prickly sensation in the nape of Frances' neck, alerting her once again to something which was beginning to have more substance, but which remained persistently vague. 'Was there something in particular you were you hoping I might have found?'

'Oh, nothing in particular really,' Claudia de Leur laughed away Frances' query with a casual indifference that did not quite ring true. 'I was merely wondering.'

Frances was wondering too. What was the true purpose behind Claudia de Leur's sudden desire to visit Thorndale? Had she been motivated by nostalgia, or was it something more fundamental?

They returned to the lounge where Megan was pouring the tea, and Claudia seated herself in a chair close to Byron. They exchanged smiles, Claudia's openly inviting, and Frances forced herself to sit down and drink her tea even though she was fuming inwardly with an emotion which she was being forced to acknowledge as jealousy. Byron turned his head at that moment to look at Frances, and that hint of amusement in his eyes was disquieting, but it was he who looked away when Claudia de Leur slid her hand along his tanned forearm to draw his attention to something she had to say.

The conversation was like thick custard, it refused to flow, and when they finally rose to leave Claudia glanced briefly once again at the portrait of George Wilkins. Frances could not be sure, but she thought she saw a flicker of anger in Claudia's grey, mascaraed eyes, and George Wilkins seemed to stare back at his niece with a look of disdain on his bearded face.

It was incredible how the facial expressions in that portrait appeared to change to suit the occasion, Frances found herself thinking after Byron and Claudia de Leur had left. It could, of course, be attributed to her own frame of mind, but at times it made her feel quite eerie.

Frances barely slept the first three nights after the lions had been introduced into the park. The roar of the male rending the silence sent shivers of apprehension cascading through her, and Sipho's warning the Friday of that same week was simply an echo of her own fears.

'*Ibhubesi lizozidla izinkomo zakho,*' he had said, his eyes wide and fearful. The lion will eat your cattle. He had seen them with his own eyes wandering beyond the high security fence near the river camp where she kept her Brahman cattle, he had told her, and Frances knew that Sipho had the same terrible misgivings about what could happen if the fence was cut again.

Olivia brought Logan to Thorndale the Saturday morning to spend the weekend with Frances, and Megan chose to remain on the farm rather than spend a weekend alone at her home in Louisville while her parents were away on a two-week holiday. It was fate, perhaps, that Frances was not alone on the farm that weekend, but it was a weekend she was never to forget as long as she lived.

It was after dinner on Saturday evening when Frances and Megan seated themselves on the carpeted floor in the lounge to play Scrabble with Logan. Major had been barking incessantly since early that evening and, in sheer desperation to silence him, Frances finally allowed him into the house. He slumped down on the floor at Frances' side, but every so often he would emit a low growl which would make Pickles, Megan's Maltese poodle, raise her head sleepily to give him an indignant stare. There was a strange uneasiness in the air that evening which Frances could not shake off, and it came almost as a relief when a loud, anxious banging on a door made Major howl excitedly as he raced out of the room. Pickles looked up sleepily, decided not to bother, and went back to sleep while Megan followed Frances and Logan out of the lounge and into the kitchen where Major was howling at the door.

'*Nkosazana!*' Sipho cried hoarsely, ashen-faced, and shaking from head to foot when Frances flung open the kitchen door to find him on the doorstep. '*Ibhubesi libulele inkomazi yakho!*'

Frances felt the blood drain away from her face to leave her cheeks feeling prickly. Her worst fears had been realised, and the nightmares had become a reality.

'What's he saying?' Megan demanded anxiously, her arm sliding protectively about Logan's shoulders and her face paling in sheer anticipation of the news Sipho had delivered. 'What's he saying, for heaven's sake?'

'A lion has killed one of my cows,' Frances interpreted, her own striking features white with shock and anger. 'I'll get my rifle.'

'*Ubobiza uyihlo,*' advised Sipho, stopping Frances in her tracks before she could leave the kitchen.

'There isn't time to call my father, Sipho,' she told her *Induna* curtly. 'Wait for me in the Land Rover, and I'll be with you as quick as I can.'

'This isn't something you can take care of single-handed,' argued Megan, her blue eyes wide and anxious in her white face when she followed Frances out of the kitchen and into the study with Logan racing at their heels. 'You can't go after the lion on your own, Frances!'

'I can, and I will!' Frances snapped, taking the .303 rifle out of the gun safe and slipping six cartridges into the magazine.

'You could be killed!' shrieked Megan in protest, her eyes dilating in horror as she stared at the rifle Frances was handling with such expertise. 'For heaven's sake, think of that!'

'All I can think of at the moment is that one of my Brahman heifers has been killed,' Frances explained tersely and, clutching the powerful rifle in her hand, she strode purposefully out of the study with Megan and Logan following at a near-running pace behind her. 'Get in touch with Byron,' she instructed Megan, speaking over her shoulder without stopping, 'and, for goodness' sake, keep Major in the house. I don't want him following me and getting in the way.'

'I'm going with you, Frances,' Logan spoke for the first time when Frances was about to leave the house.

'Oh, no, you're not!' she contradicted him sharply, but she saw her own stubbornness mirrored in his upturned face.

'If you don't take me with you, I'll saddle up a horse and ride out to the river camp on my own,' he insisted, and Frances felt herself shudder inwardly at the thought of how Olivia and her father would react if anything happened to Logan.

'Come on, then,' she agreed sternly and impatiently as she looked down into his grey eyes which were so like Olivia's. 'But I warn you, you'll have me to deal with if you move your butt out of the Land Rover. Is that understood?'

'Yes,' he nodded gravely.

'Let's go, then,' she said, but Megan placed a detaining hand on her arm.

'Frances . . .'

'Don't worry, Megan.' Frances' features were set with grim determination as she reassured her cousin. 'I know how to use this rifle, and I'll use it if I have to.'

She stepped outside, walking at a brisk pace to where she had parked the Land Rover, and Logan was close beside her. It was a dark night, and she could hear for the first time the distraught bellowing of the cattle, while the male lion roared intermittently. To visitors at Izilwane the roar of a lion might represent the exciting 'call of nature', but for Frances it represented an awakening of fear, and it made the blood run cold in her veins.

Sipho explained during the drive to the river camp how he had gone to investigate the unrest amongst the Brahman cattle, and the bellowing, restless animals had made him suspect that the fence had been cut, allowing the lion to get in. He had not seen one of the cattle being killed in the camp, but he was convinced that this is what had occurred.

Frances listened to him in silence, her hands clenched on the steering wheel and her foot hard on the accelerator, but she heard only a part of what Sipho was saying as she stared grimly ahead of her to where the powerful headlights of the Land Rover were slicing through the inky darkness. She was angry, she was also afraid, and she could not decide which emotion was dominant.

It seemed to take hours instead of minutes to reach the gate at the entrance to the river camp, and the Brahman cattle looked like ghosts in the headlights with their white bodies and glowing, frightened eyes. Their bellowing ceased as if they knew that help had arrived, and during the eerie silence that followed they could hear the lioness grunt, calling her mate, and her grunt was followed seconds later by the roaring response of the male some distance away. Frances could feel the hair rising in the nape of her neck, and she had difficulty in suppressing the shiver that raced through her body.

'I'll get out and open the gate for you, Frances,' Logan offered his assistance fearlessly.

'No, you will not!' she rejected his offer sharply, taking the rifle with her as she got out of the Land Rover. 'You will stay where you are, and that's an order!'

Logan protested loudly, but he did as he was told and remained in the vehicle while Frances and Sipho approached the gate warily and opened it.

They did some rapid counting while the white, ghostly-looking cattle almost trampled each other in their haste to get through the gate to safety, and they both ended with the same distressing figure. They were one Brahman short!

Frances was grim-faced and trembling inwardly when they got back into the Land Rover. She drove slowly through the camp, her nerves stretched almost to breaking point, and her heart beating hard and fast against her ribs while her searching glance scanned the area where the strong headlights of the Land Rover pierced the darkness. Frances was not sure afterwards which one of them saw the lion first, or whether the three of them saw it simultaneously, but it was Sipho who shattered the silence in an anxious voice.

'There, *Nkosazana*!' he said, pointing unnecessarily in the direction in which all three of them were staring. 'There is *ibhubesi*!'

Frances put her foot down hard on the brake, and shifted the gear lever into neutral before she pulled up the handbrake, but she left the engine running to prevent the headlights from dimming.

'*Gosh!*' whispered Logan excitedly into her ear as he leaned over the back of her seat. '*A real lion!*'

'*Shut up!*' she hissed back at her young brother without taking her eyes off the lioness trapped in the beam of the vehicle's lights.

The lioness had been attempting, unsuccessfully, to drag her kill towards the gaping opening in the fence, and it was possibly her failure to do this which now made her crouch in a menacing attitude behind the carcase of a Brahman heifer.

It was the lioness with the torn ear, her yellow eyes glowing with the fierce fire that made Frances quiver once again like a trapped animal in fear of its life, and she could feel her blood turn to iced water in her veins at the sound of the male lion roaring at close range.

'*Ingonyama* is calling his mate,' Sipho whispered fearfully, his hands clutching a short spear which Frances had not noticed until that moment. 'He is telling her that he is hungry.'

'She's killed a heifer that was heavily in calf,' Frances murmured, her mouth tightening, and at that moment her anger seemed to overshadow her fear as she grasped the barrel of the rifle with one hand and reached for the door handle with the other. '*Damn*, I knew I was going to have trouble with that lion.'

'Where are you going?' Logan demanded anxiously when Frances eased herself out of the Land Rover on legs that were shaky beneath her weight.

'I'm going to fire a shot into the air to frighten her, and I'm hoping she'll have the sense to leave her kill and return to the game park where the male is calling her.'

There was no sense in denying to herself that she was scared almost out of her mind. It was one thing to confront a lion through the bars of a crate, but it was a totally different matter when you found yourself facing a temperamental, savage animal across a space of twenty metres with nothing between you but the cool night air.

Frances' palms were damp as she shouldered the rifle and, for that fraction of a second when she had moved her eyes, the lioness lived up to her unpredictable nature.

'*Nkosazana!*' Sipho shouted a terrified warning, and she heard rather than saw her trusted *Induna* jump out of the Land Rover.

Frances' eyes had become riveted to the large cat leaping over the carcase of the heifer. It was charging directly at her, muscles rippling beneath the smooth, tawny coat, bloody fangs bared, and yellow eyes glowing with a fierce hatred of the one who had intruded on her kill.

The icy hand of death clutched at her, numbing her brain, but the subconscious instinct for survival took over, and she raised her rifle almost at the same time that she heard Logan shout, '*Shoot, Frances!*'

It all happened so fast that it felt as if there was barely time for anything other than blind judgement. The butt of the rifle slammed into her shoulder as her finger tightened about the trigger, and the deafening report echoed repeatedly across the silent veld while the lioness seemed to freeze in mid-air before she dropped to the ground less than five metres away from Frances. The bullet had entered her head directly between the eyes that were now staring sightlessly into the night.

Sipho uttered a warlike cry and, spear raised, he stormed at the lifeless body of the lioness.

'No, Sipho! No!' shouted Frances before the short spear could gore the heart of the beast. 'She's dead! Leave her alone!'

Sipho stepped back, lowering his spear reluctantly, and at that moment Frances became aware of Logan standing beside her. He had been there beside her when she had fired the shot that killed the lioness, she knew that now, and the mere thought of what might have happened made her turn on him furiously.

'I thought I told you not to move out of the Land Rover?' she demanded, and his grey eyes fell before hers.

'You're my sister,' he explained, 'and I couldn't let you stand here alone while the lion was charging.'

Frances stared down at the tall, sturdy and fearless ten-year-old, and her anger drained away from her. She propped her rifle against the Land Rover and pulled him into her arms to rest her cheek against his auburn head.

They were still standing there clinging to each other when a Land Rover sped through the gap in the fence and came to a bucking halt a few metres away from them. Byron leapt out of the vehicle and walked with long, angry strides towards the lifeless body of the lioness he had brought to Izilwane only a few days ago in her truck.

'My God!' he exclaimed, going down on his haunches to examine the spot where the bullet had entered the animal. 'What the *hell* did you think you were doing!'

CHAPTER EIGHT

'WHAT the *hell* did you think you were doing!'

Byron's voice echoed harshly all around her, and for the first time in her life, Frances was rendered speechless. Her brain felt numb, as if it had shifted into neutral, and she stared blankly and rather stupidly at Byron with her arm still draped about Logan's shoulders.

'I could have darted the lioness, and in that way she could have been removed without further harm being done, but *no*!' Byron's rugged features caught in the crossbeam of lights between the two parked vehicles, were etched in fury, and there was a hint of savagery in the tightness about his mouth that made his unexpected attack all the more frightening. 'You couldn't wait, could you, Frances! You never stopped for one moment to consider the cost involved because all you could think of was shooting her in retaliation. She killed one of your heifers, so *you* killed *her*! Well, congratulations!' he snarled savagely. 'You've proved your expertise with a rifle, so I'll have the hide cured and the head stuffed for you as a trophy!'

Frances was aware of a stab of pain intruding on her numbness when a vehicle sped towards them, bumping and swaying across the uneven veld, and she felt the tremors start deep down inside her when she recognised her father's Land Rover.

Bernard King leapt out of his parked vehicle with an agility not usual in a man of his age, and came striding towards them with his brows drawn together in a frown above dark eyes that narrowed perceptibly when they settled on the lifeless body of the lioness.

'What happened?' he demanded, his deep, thundering voice laced with anxiety, and Frances felt the tension snap inside her to leave her shaking like a leaf and close to tears in her father's solid, comforting presence.

'One shot, Dad!' Logan intervened, his voice ringing with admiration and excitement as he left Frances' side to approach his father. 'Just one shot and the lion was dead!'

'Quiet, Logan!' Bernard King placed a restraining hand on his son's shoulder, and his narrowed gaze shifted from Frances to Byron and back again to Frances. 'I would like to know what happened to necessitate the killing of this animal?' he demanded, gesturing towards the tawny body lying a few metres away from them.

'I would like an answer to that myself,' Byron shifted the responsibility on to Frances.

His eyes were hard, and his mouth tight with an anger he made no attempt to hide in front of her father while he waited for her to speak.

'I—I got out of the Land Rover to—to fire a warning shot into the air,' she finally explained, choking back the tears which she was determined not to shed in front of Byron, but she was shaking so much that she had difficulty in speaking. 'I wanted to frighten her away in—in the hope that she—she would return to the park, but she charged the—the minute she saw me. There wasn't time to get—get back into the Land Rover, and I—I had to shoot her. Oh, Dad!' Her voice broke humiliatingly, and she went into her father's arms to bury her face against his broad, comforting chest. 'I—I don't think I've ever been so scared in all my life!' she heard herself admitting in a muffled voice.

'It's all over now,' her father murmured soothingly, releasing her when she had succeeded in controlling those terrible tremors coursing through her body. 'I suggest you get back to the house. Olivia is there, and she'll be anxious to know that both you and Logan are safe.'

Frances nodded, she was in no fit state to argue and, taking Logan with her, she gestured to her *Induna*, who was looking at her now with a new respect in eyes that were still like saucers in his dark face.

'Come, Sipho,' she instructed. 'I'll drop you off at your house on my way home.'

'*Yebo, Nkosazana.*'

'I'll have the carcase of the heifer removed and buried for you,' offered Byron, but Frances did not answer him.

She picked up her rifle and got into her Land Rover without looking at him, but she could feel his eyes boring into her until she had the curious sensation that her flesh was burning.

She left Sipho with his wife and family, and drove home. Logan could not stop talking about what had happened, but she did not hear a word he was saying. She was thinking about how she had endangered her own life as well as Logan's, and she was thinking of the angry accusations Byron had flung at her.

She garaged the Land Rover, and they were walking through the darkness towards the house when the kitchen door opened and Olivia and Megan rushed out to meet them with Major racing ahead with a sharp, excited yelp.

'Frances! Logan! Thank God you're both safe!' Olivia exclaimed, tears of relief swamping her eyes as she embraced them both, but a look of anxiety flashed across her sensitive features the next instant. 'Where's your father?'

'He stayed behind with Byron,' Frances reassured her, trying to control the tremors that had started up inside her again as they entered the house.

'Don't be mad at me, Frances,' Megan pleaded anxiously some minutes later when Frances returned to the kitchen after storing the rifle away safely. 'I was so scared for your sake that I had to let your father know what was going on.'

'I'm not mad at you,' Frances reassured her cousin. 'I can only thank you, because my father arrived at a moment when I needed him most.'

'You should have seen it, Mom!' Logan confronted Olivia, his grey eyes alight with admiration as he seated himself on a kitchen chair beside his mother. 'Frances was terrific!'

He did not need prompting to go into detail about what had occurred that evening at the river camp, and he did it so vividly that the entire episode spilled across the screen of Frances' mind, forcing her to live through that fearful moment once again when the lioness charged.

'Just a moment, Logan,' Olivia interrupted her son to look up at Frances with concern in her grey eyes. 'Are you feeling all right, darling?'

'I'm fine, I——' Frances broke off her reply with a self-conscious laugh, and she leaned forward to grasp the edge of the wooden table for support. 'I'm a bit shaken, that's all.'

'It's all right to cry, you know,' Olivia announced quietly, and something snapped inside Frances to release the tears she had kept so firmly in check.

'Oh, Olivia!' she cried in a choked voice, sinking to the floor beside Olivia's chair and burying her face in the arms she rested in Olivia's lap.

Her tears were as stormy as a flood, and it left her drained. Her eyes were red, and her eyelids swollen, but she felt considerably calmer now that some of the tension had left her body.

'I still think you're terrific,' Logan assured her when she had wiped her eyes and blown her nose, and she was hugging him with a shaky laugh when her father walked into the kitchen.

'Is everything okay?' Bernard King asked, surveying the scene in front of him with a worried frown creasing his brow.

'Everything is fine, darling.' Olivia smiled reassuringly into her husband's anxious face. 'A few tears can do wonders for a woman to ease the tension!'

Megan poured coffee for everyone, and they fortunately did not hold a post-mortem on what had occurred. 'I'm glad I taught you how to use a rifle, Frances,' was all Bernard King said before he and Olivia left to return to Mountain View where Janet had been left in Evalina's care.

Logan went to bed, but Frances and Megan sat talking quietly in the kitchen about everything and anything which did not relate to the events of that evening. Eventually Megan yawned and glanced at her watch.

'It's ten o'clock, and I'm exhausted,' she announced, stifling yet another yawn behind her fingers as she pushed back her chair and rose tiredly to her feet.

They said 'good night', but Frances was still too shaken about what had occurred to think of going to sleep, and she decided to wade through a pile of paperwork in her study in the hope that it would take her mind off everything.

She succeeded in becoming so engrossed in what she was doing that she never heard a vehicle approaching the house, and a light tap on the study door made her look up with a start to see a sleepy Megan standing there in her towelling gown.

'You have a visitor, Frances,' Megan announced in a whisper, looking decidedly uncomfortable.

'Who is——' Frances cut her query short when Megan moved aside to make way for Byron's tall, bulky frame, and she felt herself stiffen with resentment and anger as she rose behind her desk. 'What do you want?' she demanded coldly.

'I have to talk to you,' he said, nodding his thanks to Megan as he entered the study and closed the door behind him, and Frances had a claustrophobic feeling that the room had shrunk to the size of a cupboard.

'We don't have anything to say to each other,' she argued, avoiding the probing intensity of his tawny eyes, and doing her best to ignore that aura of raw masculinity which was making her pulse quicken to an uncomfortable pace.

'I owe you an apology, Frances.'

'You owe me nothing except the courtesy of leaving my house, and leaving *me* alone in future!'

The words spilled from her lips as if she was standing apart from herself, and no longer in control while she was listening and observing her dispassionate behaviour with a vague feeling of shock.

'You don't mean that,' Byron broke the tense, strained silence between them as they stood facing each other across the width of her desk like sparring partners in an arena.

'I *do* mean it!' she insisted, flinging her pen down on to her desk in a fury as she recalled his accusations, and moving away from him to stare out of the window, but the only thing she saw was her own reflection in the glass panes. 'I'm also going to the police first thing in the morning to report the fact that the confounded fence is continually being cut between our properties.'

'I wouldn't do that if I were you,' he warned. 'I've been carrying out my own investigation, and I have a few strong leads to work on. The culprit might take fright if the police start swarming about the place, and we might lose the opportunity of bringing him to justice.'

'Who are you accusing this time?' she asked sarcastically, turning to find him standing less than a pace away from her, and her heart leapt wildly in her breast.

'Frances . . .' he began, his eyes creasing in a smile as he reached for her, but she backed away from him sharply, knowing that she would be lost if he so much as laid a finger on her.

'Don't touch me!' she snapped, her dark eyes blazing with a pain and fury he would never understand, and bitterness curved her mouth as she turned from him to walk towards her desk. 'There's one final matter to be settled between us, and I'd like to do so now before you leave.'

His dark brows drew together in a frown above narrowed, tawny eyes which no longer smiled as he watched her seat herself behind her desk and pick up her pen.

'What are you talking about?' he demanded, his deep, gravelly voice as threatening as the rumble of distant thunder.

'I want to reimburse you for the lion I shot,' she enlightened him in a cold, businesslike voice, reaching for her cheque book and opening it. 'How much do I owe you?'

He was beside her in an instant, a strange whiteness about his mouth, and his rugged features distorted with a fury she had never witnessed in anyone before.

'*Dammit*, I don't want your money!' he roared, making her jump nervously, and narrowly missing her fingers when he slammed his clenched fist down on to her cheque book with a force that made the desk shudder. 'You're the most hot-headed and stubborn individual I've ever met! You meddled in something this evening which you have absolutely no knowledge of, almost getting yourself killed in the process, and now you have the damn nerve to offer me money, as if money would——' He broke off abruptly, the whiteness about his mouth spreading across his cheekbones to make his eyes look like two flaming coals in his face as he spun her swivel chair round, and yanked her out of it to crush her against his massive chest with arms that were clamped like steel cables about her body. 'My God, I could thrash you!'

For the second time that evening Frances found herself in the grip of a totally unexpected attack, but on this occasion she had no time to defend herself, or to make him understand that her presence in the river camp that evening had been the result of her rightful interest in the welfare of her cattle, and a misguided concern for his lion. She was given no opportunity to say anything before Byron's mouth clamped down on hers with a brutal force that crushed her lips against her teeth, and the pain of it made her moan deep down in her throat while hot tears gathered behind her closed eyelids. Her body was taut with resistance, but she was rendered helpless with her arms pinned firmly at her sides, and the punishment seemed to continue for an eternity until, incredibly, she felt a wild response rising within her. She went limp against him, her mind spinning out of control, and at that moment he released her, thrusting her back into her chair with a force that almost made it topple beneath her.

'I'll stay out of your way in future,' he said, the flat finality in his harsh voice grating across raw, tender nerves as he strode towards the study door and opened it. 'Please have the courtesy to do the same for me.'

Frances sat there staring blindly at the door he had closed behind him, and she listened distractedly to his heavy footsteps growing fainter as he walked through the house. His forceful presence still lingered in her study, but the sound of his Land Rover being driven away at speed seemed to sever that fragile link, and her slim shoulders started to shake with the convulsive sobs emerging from her throat while stinging tears spilled down her pale cheeks.

What had she done? Oh, God, what had she done? She had sent him out of her life in a fit of temper, and he had taken her at her word. She fingered her bruised, throbbing lips, and a renewed bout of tears spilled from her lashes on to her cheeks. She would never have believed that being kissed in anger could bruise the soul as well as the lips, and she never wanted to be kissed like that again.

Frances saddled Pegasus at sunrise the following morning and rode out to the river camp with Major running along behind them. She took her rifle with her to assuage that jittery feeling inside her, but she found the ride refreshing and exhilarating, while the wind whipping against her face and through her hair seemed to blow away the cobwebs which had resulted from the long hours of restless tossing in her bed.

Her Brahman cattle had scattered all over the place, and they would have to be herded back into the river camp, but she had to make sure that nothing had been left behind to remind the cattle of what had happened the night before.

The gate into the river camp was still open, and Frances slowed Pegasus down to a trot, but Major let out an eerie howl and sped ahead with his nose to the ground. The carcases of the heifer and the lioness had been removed, as Byron had promised, but Frances gave the area where they had lain a wide berth to check whether the fence had been repaired. It had, and her fingers slackened their hold on the rifle, making her realise how nervous she had actually been. She had not wanted to go anywhere near the place where she had shot the lioness, but she somehow found herself steering Pegasus in that direction.

A shiver raced through her when she reached it, but there was nothing there to remind her of what had occurred other than the fresh imprint of truck tyres in the dew-wet earth. Byron must have had a team of his workers there very early that morning to remove the two carcases.

Byron! She did not want to think of Byron. She had thought about him all night, but now she had to put him out of her mind, and she had no idea how she was going to accomplish that.

The sound of an approaching horse made her look up to see Tony riding towards her on his Arab stallion, and she had to control her features to hide the fact that she was not in the mood for his company.

'I've only just heard about what happened last night,' he explained the reason for his presence at that early hour of the morning when he reined in beside her and cast a quick glance about the camp.

'The news has obviously travelled fast,' she murmured drily.

'You know what the herdsmen are like,' he smiled.

'They talk among themselves, and they admire you as much as I do for your marksmanship. Facing a charging lion and killing it with one shot is quite a feat for a woman whose femininity is inclined to make men believe she wouldn't know which end of a rifle to fire from.'

'Is that supposed to be a compliment?' she asked, attempting to look amused but failing as she urged Pegasus away from the spot where the lioness with the torn ear had lain after that fatal bullet had entered her head.

'I think you were very brave, Frances,' Tony answered her gravely, urging his own horse into a slow walk in the direction of the gate, 'and I don't think it was nice of Rockford to give you such a tough time afterwards.'

'So you've heard about that too, have you?' she smiled with a hint of cynicism curving her lovely mouth.

'I can imagine Rockford wasn't exactly thrilled about one of his lions being shot, but under the circumstances one would think that he would have understood that you had no choice.'

Frances did not want to be reminded of the angry words which had passed between Byron and herself the previous evening, and she changed the subject. 'Are you aware that your cousin, Claudia de Leur, is staying at Izilwane?'

A strange look flashed across Tony's handsome face at the mention of his cousin's name, but it was gone before Frances could analyse it.

'She telephoned me the same day she arrived at Izilwane,' he said, smiling twistedly. 'She had some crazy idea that we ought to contest my uncle's will, but I told her it would be a waste of time. The lawyer had made it quite clear after my uncle's death that the will was perfectly legal, and that my uncle had been in possession of all his faculties when it was drawn up.'

Frances could not conceal her start of surprise, and she glanced sharply at the fair-haired man seated on the Arab stallion which was beginning to show signs of restlessness at being reined in to a walk. 'You thought of contesting his will?'

'Yes,' he admitted, a hint of cynicism curving his mouth, and a hardness in his hazel eyes which she had never noticed before. 'I very seriously considered contesting his will when I discovered that he'd left instructions for the farm to be sold and the proceeds donated to some stupid charity. Wouldn't you have done the same if you had been in my position?'

Frances could not answer him. She felt a little sick inside at the knowledge that Tony could have questioned his uncle's decision, and his sanity, but she also found herself wondering at the reason behind George Wilkins' wish to sell his farm rather than leave it to his family.

They parted company at the river camp's gate with Frances muttering something about Megan and Logan wondering about her absence at the breakfast table and, calling Major to heel, she rode back to the house.

Her mind was in a turmoil with thoughts coming and going, and none of them making sense. She was tired. She had wrestled all night with one problem, and now she was burdening her mind with yet another. It was too much, and it would have driven her crazy if her father, Olivia and Janet had not arrived at Thorndale during the course of that morning to spend the rest of the Sunday with Megan and herself.

Logan had to give his sister a detailed account of what had occurred the previous evening, and Janet was a bundle of indignation at having missed out on the fun. *Fun!* Facing a ferocious, charging lioness was not exactly Frances' idea of *fun*, but the look on her little sister's face made her laugh, and the atmosphere lightened considerably when the rest of the family joined in, their laughter easing the tension which had plagued them all since the night before.

The roar of the lion seemed to come from a greater distance that evening when Frances and Megan sat drinking their coffee in the lounge after dinner. It was

possible that the two remaining lions had been frightened away by the shot she had fired, and had moved to a
different territory in the game park, but Frances was not
thinking about the lions that evening. She was staring at
the portrait of George Wilkins, and wondering what
secrets lay behind that benign smile he appeared to
bestow on her that evening.

'Why didn't you leave the farm to Tony and Claudia?'
Frances voiced her query out loud, and she smiled when
the old man's expression seemed to become shuttered.
'Okay, you don't have to tell me, but I'll find the answer
sooner or later.'

'That is an extraordinary portrait,' Megan remarked,
placing her empty cup in the tray and rising to examine
the portrait at close range. 'His expressions seem to alter
to suit every mood.'

'I'm relieved to know that you've noticed it too,
because I was beginning to think that I'm going crazy,'
Frances laughed self-consciously.

'The frame fascinates me most,' murmured Megan,
taking the portrait off the wall and carrying it to her chair
where she sat running her fingers along the edges of the
intricate design impressed on the metal frame. 'It's so
totally out of the ordinary,'

Frances leaned back in her chair, closing her eyes as
she stretched her long, shapely legs out in front of her,
and a tired sigh passed her lips. 'Hm, I can't help
wondering about——'

A soft, jarring 'click' interrupted her, scattering her
thoughts, and it was followed almost at once by Megan's
startled voice whispering, 'Hey, will you come and take a
look at this!'

What Frances saw was something that belonged in a
mystery novel, and not in real life. The four sections of
the square metal frame had snapped back like lids to
reveal neat piles of ten-rand notes stashed away carefully
in the hollow sections, and she stared at it, speechless
with surprise.

'Look, I'll show you,' Megan demonstrated her discovery to her incredulous cousin.

She snapped the sections back into their former position. Then, as she exerted a little pressure on a raised area in the bottom right-hand corner of the frame, the four sections leapt open again like trapdoors that had been sprung. Surrounded by all those neat stacks of banknotes, George Wilkins looked as if he was smiling smugly into his whiskers, and an answering smile lifted the corners of Frances' mouth as she recognised the cleverness of the man in the portrait.

'What are you smiling about?' demanded Megan when she raised her glance to observe Frances with a curious look in her blue eyes.

'I'm wondering what Tony and his cousin Claudia de Leur will say when they discover what it is they turned down when they were so adamant about not wanting their uncle's portrait,' Frances explained, her smile deepening.

Megan smiled back at her, but her expression sobered when she glanced down at the portrait resting on her knees, and she gestured vaguely with her hands. 'I wonder what all this amounts to.'

'I don't think I want to count it,' Frances answered her with a measure of distaste, and an odd feeling that she might defile the old man's memory by handling the money he had hidden there.

A memory, not many days old, flashed into her mind like a movie on to a screen. She could see Claudia de Leur running her manicured fingers along the carved edge of the desk which had belonged to her uncle, and Frances wondered if Claudia had perhaps suspected that her uncle had hidden a large amount of money somewhere in, or amongst, his possessions. No, that was a ridiculous thought! she chided herself.

'What are you going to do with the money?' Megan's practical query intruded on her thoughts and forced her to think rationally.

'For the moment, I think, we'll leave the money where it is,' she decided, 'but first thing tomorrow morning I'm taking the portrait to Thomas Atherstone, and I hope he'll know what to do with its contents.'

A puzzled frown creased Megan's smooth brow as she snapped the sections of the frame back into position and returned the portrait to its position against the wall. 'I wonder why he hid the money in the frame of his portrait.'

'I'm wondering that myself,' Frances admitted, but she was beginning to suspect that George Wilkins had been a disillusioned and disappointed old man.

The portrait of George Wilkins lay on Thomas Atherstone's desk with its frame emptied of its contents, and the lawyer was counting softly, his fingers moving rapidly through each pile of bank notes.

'Incredible!' he murmured at length, leaning back in his swivel chair and brushing a hand over his balding head. 'There's fifty thousand rand here.'

Frances' dark eyes widened perceptibly, and there was a slight tremor in her hands when she unnecessarily smoothed the skirt of her blue and grey floral suit over her shapely thighs. 'Why would George Wilkins have hidden a large sum of money like that in the frame of his portrait?'

'He never had complete faith in banks, and he was always stashing money away somewhere,' Thomas Atherstone explained with an amused smile creasing his lean face. 'He was also a great inventor of gadgets, and he once installed a secret compartment in the side panelling of his desk, but he did away with that some years ago by replacing the false panel with a solid one.'

Frances felt her insides jolt, and something clicked in her mind. Claudia had known of the existence of that false panel in the desk.

Thomas Atherstone stared thoughtfully at the portrait, his elbows resting on the arms of his chair and his fingertips pressed together. 'You say you offered this portrait to Tony Phillips and Claudia de Leur?'

'Yes,' she confirmed, 'and neither of them wanted it.'

'You know, Frances, there was something George Wilkins made me add into his will which I never fully understood, and which the eccentric old man refused to explain.' Thomas Atherstone rose behind his desk to open his safe, and took out a legal document which he paged through rapidly. 'Ah, yes, here it is.'

'What does it say?'

'It says simply, "The one who cares for my memory will be rewarded".' The lawyer was smiling when he returned the document to the safe and seated himself behind the desk. 'I think I understand it now. Tony and Claudia were both given the opportunity to reap this reward, but they turned it down because they didn't care enough about their uncle, but you, a stranger, cared for his memory, Frances. You kept the portrait when you could have discarded it, so the reward is yours.'

Frances stared at the lawyer incredulously. 'Are you saying that George Wilkins hid that money in the frame of his portrait for the purpose of testing the depth of his niece's and nephew's affection?'

'That's exactly what I'm saying,' Thomas Atherstone nodded, 'and they failed the test hopelessly.'

Frances was shaken by this disclosure, and it took a moment before she could think rationally to recall the conversation she had had with Tony the previous day. 'Tony told me that the proceeds from the sale of the farm had to be donated to a charity.'

'That's correct,' the lawyer confirmed. 'It's been paid into a fund towards the erection of a home for the aged in Louisville.'

That was a noble gesture from a noble man, Frances thought, and it came as a shock to recall that Tony had referred to a home for the aged as a *stupid charity*.

'I would like you to add this amount to the fund as a

donation from Megan and myself,' she voiced her decision.

'Are you sure that's what you want?'

'Absolutely sure,' she nodded emphatically, glancing at the portrait, and she could almost swear that she saw approval in the eyes staring back at her beneath the white, bushy eyebrows.

'You're very generous, Frances,' the lawyer said gravely, but a teasing light entered his eyes when she rose to wrap the portrait in strong brown paper. 'I believe you had a spot of bother with a lion on your farm the other night, and that you have a deadly accurate aim with a rifle.'

'I'd rather not discuss that, if you don't mind,' Frances answered him solemnly while she secured the wrapping with string, and prepared to leave his office. 'It was something that should never have happened.'

She left Thomas Atherstone's office with the portrait clutched under her arm, and when she stepped out of the stone building she could not decide whether the portrait felt lighter, or whether it was simply her own frame of mind which had lightened.

'Frances!' The voice was familiar, and it wrenched at her heart as nothing had ever done before to make her pause briefly in her stride to glance over her shoulder. Byron was crossing the street, and his grey slacks and white shirt accentuated the width of his massive shoulders and the leanness of his hips. He was striding purposefully towards her, but she ignored him, and walked on with a fast beating heart to where she had parked her Land Rover. 'Frances, wait!'

She had opened the door of the Land Rover and had placed the portrait on the back seat when his hand gripped her arm, sending a shaft of feeling through her that made her stiffen.

She stared down at that sun-browned hand with the tiny dark hair on the back of it. She was loving and also hating his touch, but her expression was cool and controlled when she looked up into Byron's tawny eyes. 'I thought we'd agreed to stay out of each other's way.'

'Let's not be ridiculous about this,' he brushed aside her remark, and the sun seemed to set fire to his dark brown hair when he tilted his head at an arrogant angle. 'We were both angry and upset the other night, and we said a few regrettable things.'

That was true, but Frances was still smarting in the aftermath of what had occurred between them, and she refused to agree with him. 'I think we made it quite clear what we thought of each other.'

'Let's discuss that over a cup of tea, shall we?' he smiled faintly, closing the Land Rover's door, and tightening his grip on her arm as he ushered her towards the tearoom across the street.

CHAPTER NINE

'EASE up, Frances,' Byron instructed tersely when they sat facing each other across a table in the corner of the tearoom with two cups of tea on the red-checkered cloth in front of them. 'It's quite impossible to have a calm and rational discussion with someone who's determined not to co-operate.'

'This was your idea, not mine,' she reminded him coldly, her striking features rigid with the effort to hide her feelings.

'If I'm prepared to meet you halfway, surely you could do the same for me?' he demanded with a gleam of mockery in the eyes that held hers.

'Give me one good reason why I should,' she countered swiftly, raising her dark head proudly.

'Have you never said or done anything in anger which you regretted afterwards?' he asked, striking at the heart of her, and her resentment crumbled into dust.

'Many times,' she admitted reluctantly, lowering her gaze with a measure of shame as she brushed back a stray strand of hair, and self-consciously fingered the knot in the blue scarf that held her hair together in the nape of her neck. Her anger drained away, and she was left with the bitterness of that familiar feeling of regret he had mentioned. 'I'm sorry I had to shoot that lioness.'

'So am I,' he said, his lips twitching in response to her rueful smile as he raised his teacup and drained it.

'I wish you'd let me compensate you for your financial loss,' she touched on the subject which troubled her most, and his sensuous mouth tightened into a hard, unrelenting line.

'You came very close to being killed, Frances.' There was a hint of unbridled anger in his deep-throated voice that made her tremble inwardly. 'Do you think a cheque would have been sufficient compensation for your family, and for the people who care about you?'

She had never looked at the situation from that angle, and she considered it for a moment, shaking her head. 'No, I suppose not, but——'

'Frances,' he interrupted her sharply, leaning towards her across the small table, with an unfathomable expression in his eyes, 'I can understand and accept that it was concern which prompted you to go out to the river camp the other night, but it's a fact that, had you not interfered, I could have removed the lion from your property without it causing further harm. I can also accept that you had no option but to shoot the animal when she charged, but it was the thought of what might have happened to you that made me so unreasonably angry.'

Her heart seemed to stop beating for a moment before it raced on at a speed that made her feel dizzy. Was it possible that he was trying to make her understand that it would have mattered to him if something serious had happened to her? She stared at him without speaking, trying desperately to probe beyond the shuttered expression in his tawny eyes, but she failed hopelessly, and disappointment made her pulse rate slow down to a grinding pace.

'Byron!' The husky ejaculation cut across the pleasant murmur of the patrons' voices and the rattle of teacups, and Frances looked up sharply, only barely concealing her displeasure when she saw Claudia de Leur approaching their table. 'Darling!' Claudia smiled at Byron as he rose politely to his feet, her slender, manicured hand sliding possessively up his arm, and her pose seductive in the white slacks and yellow top which clung to her body like a second skin. 'How fortuitous that I should run into you this morning in the only tearoom this godforsaken place possesses.'

Godforsaken? Louisville? Frances felt her hackles rise,

but she bit back the angry words that rose to her lips in defence of her hometown when Claudia turned to her to acknowledge her presence with a brief nod and a coldly speculative look in her eyes.

'Good morning, Claudia,' Byron smiled at the blonde with an easy intimacy that stabbed Frances in a region where it hurt, and he drew out the vacant chair at their table. 'Won't you join us?'

'Thank you, darling,' Claudia purred, her heady perfume making Frances' nostrils flare in protest as the blonde seated herself with an affected grace. 'I'm absolutely dying for a cup of tea.'

Frances' glance met Byron's briefly when he resumed his seat, and the amusement lurking in his eyes made her stiffen with anger as he gestured to the waitress that they wanted a fresh pot of tea at their table.

'What are you doing in town this early on a Monday morning?' he questioned Claudia while they waited.

'I had to bring my car to the garage for a few minor repairs, and they couldn't tell me how long it would take,' Claudia explained with a pained expression on her beautiful face as she reached out to place her bejewelled hand on Byron's arm where it rested on the table. 'I simply can't tell you how relieved I am to know that I'm not exactly stranded, and that I can get a lift back to Izilwane with you. I'm sure you won't mind bringing me into town again later today to collect my car. You'll do that for me, won't you, darling?'

Claudia de Leur spoke with the assurance of a woman who had a physical hold on the man to whom she was speaking, and Byron seemed to confirm this when he agreed readily to Claudia's request.

'It will be a pleasure, Claudia,' he said, and Frances felt sick inside at the knowledge that a man like Byron could be so easily manipulated by a woman as shallow and grasping as Claudia de Leur.

'I knew you'd say that,' Claudia laughed gaily, pouting her crimson lips and unashamedly blowing him a kiss before she glanced at Frances. 'Isn't he just the sweetest and the darlingest man?' she asked in a honeyed voice.

'I guess that's a matter of opinion,' Frances replied stonily, and with a cynical lift of one dark eyebrow as she picked up her handbag and rose to her feet. 'Thanks for the tea, Byron.'

'Leaving so soon?' Claudia demanded of Frances with feigned disappointment. 'I was hoping you could tell me something I need to know about my dear departed uncle, but perhaps I should see you privately at the farm later today, or at some future date depending on how long it takes to repair my car.'

'You're welcome,' Frances agreed bluntly, wondering what Claudia de Leur would say if she knew the nature of the errand which had brought her to town that morning.

'Frances!' She cast a cool glance over her shoulder to see Byron murmur an apology to Claudia as he rose from the table, but did not pause in her stride as she made her way out of the crowded tearoom, and he caught up with her outside. 'I'll walk with you to your Land Rover,' he said, taking her arm and shortening his steps to match hers.

'No, thank you, Byron,' she declined his offer, her voice cold and brittle with anger as she removed her arm from his clasp. 'I'm quite capable of walking back to my vehicle on my own.'

'What the devil's got into you now?' he demanded in a low, angry growl.

'Just leave me alone, Byron!' Frances muttered through her teeth, shaking inwardly with a growing anger when she paused and turned to face him before crossing the street. 'It was a mistake to have tea with you this morning, and I think we should stick to what we decided the other night. Stay out of my way, and I'll stay out of yours!'

She crossed the street, almost running in her haste to get away from him before he noticed the glimmer of angry tears in her eyes. She was in a jealous rage; she admitted it to herself with a measure of self-disgust, but she couldn't help it!

Frances drove back to Thorndale at a speed that matched her stormy mood, and exchanged her elegant clothes for an old pair of denims and a cinnamon-coloured shirt. There was only one way she could rid herself of the anger churning through her, and that was to go for a long, hard ride, she decided, pulling on her soft leather boots.

She saddled Pegasus, and was only vaguely aware of Sipho's wide-eyed observation when she leapt on the animal's back and galloped away at a wild, reckless speed. She did not pause to wonder what Sipho must be thinking. The only thing she was conscious of was that leaden feeling in her breast, and the painful knowledge that she was in love with a man who could never love her in return.

Frances returned to the house an hour later to see Claudia de Leur's blue Toyota parked in the shade of the jacarandas, and her hands clenched spasmodically at her sides when she entered the house to find the shapely blonde seated in her lounge.

'Where is my uncle's portrait?' Claudia demanded, rising and gesturing to where the portrait had hung against the wall.

'It's still in my Land Rover,' Frances answered with a tight smile curving her mouth while she stood facing her adversary across the room, and the atmosphere was tense and bristling with an anger that emanated from Frances as well as Claudia de Leur. 'Do you want it after all?'

'Not now that you've removed from it what was rightfully mine,' Claudia declined with a smirk marring her beautiful features.

'I beg your pardon?' asked Frances, a wave of incredulity sweeping through her, and a satisfied smile replaced the smirk on the blonde's face.

'News travels fast in a small community such as this, and I went to see Mr Atherstone this morning to have the rumours confirmed,' Claudia explained with that calculating coldness in her grey eyes as she trailed a manicured hand along the back of a chair. 'I think I must have arrived at his office seconds after you left.'

'So you know about the money we found in the portrait.'

'Yes, I know.' Claudia's hand clenched on the back of the chair, and a look of unexpected fury distorted her features. 'You had no right to give away my inheritance!'

'*Your* inheritance?' A mirthless laugh escaped Frances at this woman's audacious and incongruous statement. 'It could equally have been *Tony's* inheritance, but neither of you wanted the portrait.'

'That's beside the point,' she snapped, waving aside Frances' remark. 'You had no right to take that money to the lawyer without first consulting *me* . . . or Tony,' she added the latter as a hasty afterthought.

'Thomas Atherstone was your uncle's lawyer, Mrs de Leur, and I had no intention of doing anything without first seeking his advice.'

'You've taken possession of everything else that belonged to my uncle, and you got the farm at a bargain price, I might add, Claudia accused unjustly.

'I made a fair and reasonable offer for this farm, just like everyone else, and my offer was accepted,' Frances contradicted her with a calmness she was far from experiencing. 'I wouldn't say I got it at a bargain price.'

'Wouldn't you?' Claudia smiled coldly, a spiteful, calculating look entering her eyes. 'Oh, and I also heard about how you took the money you found and donated it towards a home for the aged. That was such a *noble* gesture, but I know exactly what prompted you to do that. I know your sort, Frances King. You did it to impress Byron Rockford, because you're in love with him!'

Frances felt her insides lurch sickeningly at this woman's appalling insinuations. She was also momentarily stunned by Claudia's startling ability to her feelings for Byron with such deadly accuracy.

'You don't know what you're talking about!' she protested, but she was humiliatingly aware of the telltale warmth that came and went in her cheeks to leave her pale.

'Don't I?' Claudia smiled twistedly, a glitter of triumph in her cold grey eyes when her glance lingered briefly on Frances' faded denims and dusty boots. 'Well, I've got news for you, darling. Byron Rockford's interest lies in Thorndale, and not in *you*. He wants this farm, and he'll do anything to get it. If he can't persuade you to sell, then he might even resort to marrying you to get his hands on it!'

Frances clenched her hands at her sides as an icy coldness filtered into her veins. She wished she could ignore Claudia's remarks, but there was a frightening logic in everything she had said. Byron *was* interested in buying Thorndale, and she was in possession of his written request for first option to buy the farm if she should want to sell it. But *marriage*? Would he stoop that low to achieve his aim?

'This farm may have belonged to your uncle, Mrs de Leur, but I bought it lock, stock and barrel from his estate.' The chilling displeasure in Frances' voice stemmed from the iciness which felt as if it had penetrated deep into her soul. 'Thorndale now belongs to me, and you are no longer welcome here.'

'I'm going,' Claudia smiled with that hateful glitter of triumph still lurking in her eyes as she slipped the strap of her sling bag on to her shoulder, 'but don't say I didn't warn you.'

Frances stood aside stiffly, and Claudia swept past her with the high heels of her sandals tapping sharply on the uncarpeted sections of the floor. She heard the Toyota being driven away at speed seconds later, but Claudia's heady perfume still lingered in the lounge, and Frances' nostrils flared once again in protest.

Byron Rockford's interest lies in Thorndale. If he can't persuade you to sell, then he might even resort to marrying you to get his hands on it. Don't say I didn't warn you.

Claudia's hateful words echoed through Frances' tortured mind. She did not want to believe it, but she could not ignore the possibility that there might have been a grain of truth in Claudia's warning.

Frances clenched her hands at her sides until her nails bit into her palms, and she drew a strangled, agonised breath as she stormed out of the lounge to closet herself in her study.

The sound of a vehicle approaching the house, not fifteen minutes after Claudia had left, made Frances stiffen behind her desk. She heard Gladys' heavy, shuddering footsteps echoing through the quiet house to answer the imperious knocking on the front door, and moments later a second set of slow, heavy footsteps accompanied Gladys' in the direction of her study.

It was Byron. She knew it long before the door was flung open, and her expression was carefully controlled when she glanced up to see him entering her study with a look of dark anger on his rugged face.

'It's customary to knock when one is confronted by a closed door,' she said in a cold, accusing voice.

'I thought this morning that we'd succeeded in clearing up the misunderstandings between us, but the thought had barely entered my mind when you extended your claws for some obscure reason and started spitting like a wildcat.' He closed the door and seated himself on the corner of the desk so that his knee almost touched her hand where it rested on the arm of her chair, and his nearness was unnerving and disturbing to the senses. 'What happened, Frances?'

'Nothing happened!' she snapped, finding it difficult to avoid the probing and angry intensity of his tawny gaze.

'Did I say something to annoy you?'

'No.'

'Then what, in heaven's name, prompted that little scene in town this morning?' he exploded in a thundering voice that sent a quiver racing through her, but she concealed her feelings behind a cool aloofness.

'Let's just say I realised once again that we're like two chemical components that knock sparks of rejection off each other when we're put together, and that I honestly consider it's for the best if we stay out of each other's way as much as possible in future.'

'You're lying, Frances!' he accused harshly, his large hands taking her shoulders in a punishing grip as he rose and jerked her to her feet with him, and the pain that shot across her shoulders and down into her arms left her incapable of resisting him physically when he lowered his angry face to hers until she could feel his cool breath against her lips. 'I know we've had our disagreements, and I admit that there have been plenty of misunderstandings, but what there is between us is complementary, not destructive, and I'll prove it to you!'

'You're hurting me! Let me go!' she cried out in protest, her heart thudding wildly against her ribs, but Byron's muscled thighs brushed against hers, sending a shaft of unwanted sensations darting through her as he urged her back two paces until she was trapped between the hard wall and his equally hard body.

Frances steeled herself inwardly in preparation for the brute force of his mouth on hers, but the caressing touch of his strongly chiselled lips was shatteringly sensual, and the pain eased out of her arms when he released her shoulders to stroke her body into a vibrant and trembling awareness of a need she had only guessed at before.

The tip of his tongue traced the outline of her lips and teased the corners of her mouth until her lips parted with an eagerness for his deeper exploration. She loved him, a part of her had secretly yearned for this, and Claudia de Leur was but a fleeting shadow passing through her drugged mind at that moment.

The desire to touch him was too strong to resist, and

her hands slid up across his chest until her arms circled his neck. She responded to the passion of his kisses with a wild abandon, barely conscious of his fingers tugging at the buttons of her blouse, and unhooking the front catch of her bra to free her breasts. For one fraction of a second she was assailed by doubt as to the wisdom of what she was allowing, but it was such a fleeting thought that it was gone the next instant when his stroking, probing fingers sent a shudder of the most exquisite pleasure racing through her heated body.

'Oh, Byron!' she whispered jerkily, her fingers locked in the short, surprisingly soft hair at the nape of his neck, and he moved against her, making her aware of his heated desire when his mouth left hers to probe and explore the sensitive areas along the column of her smooth throat.

Strange things were happening to her own body, and she was beyond caring about the danger of allowing this situation to develop too far when Byron groaned softly against her throat and eased himself away from her. His hands were pressed flat against the wall on either side of her head, and he was not breathing normally when he leaned his damp forehead lightly against hers for a moment. Her own breath was passing her lips in an unfamiliar, jerky manner, and she was aware that she was trembling violently with the intensity of the emotions and unfulfilled desires he had aroused in her.

'What do you have to say for yourself now?' he murmured, a smile curving his mouth, and through the open window the shrill sound of the cicadas in the jacarandas found a sobering echo deep down inside her that filled her with shame.

She ducked swiftly under his arm, and turned her back on him while she fastened the catch of her bra and buttoned up her blouse with fingers that shook. Her cheeks were flaming, but a coldness was beginning to invade her body, and it was reflected in her voice when she answered him.

'The only thing you have proved is that we're capable of arousing each other physically, and something that's purely physical is bound to be destructive.'

She heard him draw an angry breath, and his hand was heavy on her shoulder when he spun her round to face him. 'Dammit, Frances, I want to marry you!'

She could feel the blood draining out of her cheeks to leave her deathly pale. She had not wanted to believe that the man she loved could demean himself in this way, and an icy rage erupted inside her to overshadow the blinding pain of her discovery. How could she have misjudged him so badly?

'I'm not in the market for marriage, and most certainly not to a man who considers that it's the only way he can get his hands on my property!' her chilling rejection spilled from her lips, and Byron's tawny eyes narrowed to a hard glitter as a pasty whiteness seeped beneath the healthy tan on his rugged cheeks.

'Is that what you believe?'

Defend yourself! she wanted to shout at him. *Tell me it isn't true*! But instead, she turned from him and crossed the room to stare blindly out of the window with a bitter cynicism curving her mouth when she said, 'After Claudia's timely warning, what else am I to believe?'

'When did Claudia issue this warning?' he asked quietly, but his voice had an ominous ring to it that made her turn to face him curiously.

'She left here about fifteen minutes before you arrived,' she answered him, her dark eyes searching, but she could not probe beneath his cold, shuttered expression.

Something was wrong, she could feel it in the air between them, and it was beginning to frighten her, but she could not put a name to it. What *was* it?

'You're an intelligent woman, Frances,' Byron was saying, 'but if you choose to believe someone like Claudia de Leur, then you and I have nothing more to say to each other.'

Frances encountered the oddest feeling while she watched him walk away from her, and it rose like a fountain inside her until it seemed to explode into her tormented mind. It was doubt! She was doubting the validity of Claudia's statement, but she had to be absolutely sure, and Byron was the only one who could give her that assurance.

She raised a pleading hand as she took a halting step in his direction to detain him. 'Byron, I think I——'

'You were right, Frances,' he cut harshly across her plea, halting her in her stride when he turned for her to see his rugged features etched in hard, forbidding lines. 'We are two destructive components when we're put together, and the only solution to the problem is for us to stay out of each other's way.'

The flat finality in his voice was like a sword sweeping down to sever a vital cord, and Frances felt a coldness surging into her body as if she was being drained of her life's blood. She stared blindly at the door he had closed behind him, and his heavy footsteps fading through the house seemed to keep time with the slow, painful beat of her dying heart.

She had no idea how long she stood there after he had gone, but she came to her senses with the realisation that she was shaking violently, and drawing jerky gasps of air into her lungs along a tight, aching throat. She walked the few paces towards her desk to lean weakly against it with her hands pressed flat upon its surface to steady herself. Her head was bowed, her eyes stinging as her vision blurred, but she drew a shuddering breath, determined not to release those futile tears as she straightened and strode out of her study.

She was walking aimlessly through the orchard. She had no idea why she was there, or how she had got there, but she walked up between one row of fruit trees and down between another with her fingers pushed into the hip pockets of her faded denims and her nostrils quivering appreciatively with the scent of orange blossoms permeating the air. She had to keep on walking. If she stopped she knew she would fall apart.

'Frances?'

She spun round sharply to see Olivia coming towards her along the narrow avenue of orange trees, and that gentle, familiar smile on her delicate features was the most heart-warming sight at that precise moment.

'Gladys told me I would find you here, and it's such a hot day I think we ought to sit on that bench in the shade of the oak tree,' Olivia continued conversationally, linking her arm through Frances', and leading her out of the orchard.

Frances did not speak. There was no need to. Olivia was there beside her, and her calm strength seemed to flow through Frances like a soothing balm.

'I had a feeling that you needed me,' Olivia quietly explained the reason for her presence at Thorndale when they were seated on the roughly hewn bench built in a circle round the gnarled stem of the oak tree. 'Do you, darling?'

Frances nodded affirmatively, her throat too tight to speak, and her red-rimmed eyes filling with the tears which she had wanted so desperately to suppress.

'Have a good cry first, and after that we can talk if you want to,' Olivia suggested wisely, her arm sliding about Frances, and Frances turned into her arms with a choked cry to weep bitterly against the comforting shoulder she had been offered.

'Feeling better?' Olivia asked eventually, passing her a handkerchief when the storm of tears had passed.

'A little,' Frances sniffed while she dabbed at her eyes with the small square of fine, embroidered linen which bore a trace of the delicate and familiar fragrance of Olivia's perfume.

'Do you want to tell me who, or what, has upset you like this?' Olivia prompted calmly.

Frances stared blindly into the distance for a long time

before she could trust herself sufficiently to speak. 'I'm in love with Byron.'

She had not meant to say that, it had spilled of its own volition from her aching heart, and there was a surprised little silence before Olivia asked with a smile in her voice, 'Is that so terrible?'

'He doesn't love *me*! At least he never said so, and Claudia de Leur——' Frances halted abruptly to glance at her stepmother. 'You haven't met George Wilkins' niece, have you?'

'No, but I've heard about her.'

Frances sighed heavily and looked away again, staring blankly across the sun-drenched orchard as she haltingly recounted the incidents which had occurred that morning, ending with, 'Claudia guessed how I felt about Byron, and just before I ordered her out of the house she warned me that Byron's only interest was in this farm. She said he would do anything to get it and, if he couldn't persuade me to sell, he might even resort to marrying me to get it.'

'Do you believe her?'

'I did at the time,' Frances confessed in an agonised voice. 'It all sounded so logical when I recalled the way Byron had reacted when he heard that I'd bought Thorndale.'

'But?' Olivia prompted.

'I think it was terribly wrong of me to allow my judgement to be swayed by Claudia,' Frances groaned, pressing the handkerchief to her quivering lips. 'And I think I've made the biggest mistake of my life.'

'In what way?' Olivia prompted again in her calm, quiet way.

'Byron arrived here after Claudia had left. We were having a row of sorts, and then he——' The sheen of tears was in Frances' eyes, and she drew a shuddering breath in an attempt to control herself. 'He said he wanted to marry me.'

'And, his proposal coming directly after Claudia's

poisonous remarks, you naturally turned him down,'
Olivia concluded with her remarkable ability to understand and assess a situation.

'Yes, I turned him down ... and I did so in no
uncertain terms,' Frances confirmed with a bitter,
anguished laugh. 'If he'd said he loved me, then I might
still have ... oh, I don't know!' she moaned in despair,
gesturing helplessly with her hands and leaning back
against the stem of the oak.

'Men are inclined to forget that it's important to a
woman to know that she's loved, and it makes matters
worse when the woman suspects that the man she loves
has an ulterior motive for proposing.' Olivia was
thoughtful, a reminiscent smile lurking in her grey eyes,
and her smile deepened with a touch of amusement when
her glance finally met Frances'. 'I turned your father
down the first time he proposed.'

'Why?' asked Frances, knowing that she must look as
startled as she felt.

'I thought his sole purpose in asking me to marry him
was because he felt you needed a mother,' Olivia gently
voiced the revealing truth for the first time, her hand
resting lightly on Frances' arm, and Frances nodded
gravely.

'You wanted to be my mother, but you also wanted to
know that you had my father's love, is that it?'

'Yes,' Olivia confirmed, that reminiscent smile lurking
in her eyes once again, and Frances placed her hand over
Olivia's with a touch of anxiety in the grip of her fingers.

'How am I ever going to know it's *me* Byron wants, and
not Thorndale?' she cried out in anguish. '*If* he ever asks
me to marry him again, that is.'

'You'll know, darling,' Olivia assured her with a
smiling confidence which Frances was far from experiencing at that moment. 'Men like your father and Byron
Rockford have difficulty in expressing their feelings, but
when they finally allow you to see into their hearts, it's an

experience which will remain with you for the rest of your life.'

An experience which would remain with her for the rest of her life! Would she ever have that experience? Had her rejection of Byron not perhaps caused irretrievable damage to their relationship, and was she not perhaps yearning for something which would always remain beyond her reach?

'Come on, darling, let's walk back to the house,' Olivia suggested, getting up and drawing Frances to her feet. 'I've invited myself to lunch, and you'll want to wash away the trace of tears on your face before Megan arrives.'

'Olivia?' Frances lowered her head slightly to kiss her stepmother's smooth cheek. 'I'm glad you married my father because we both love you very much, and I don't know what I'd have done without you.'

'Thank you, Frances,' Olivia smiled, her grey eyes shining with a suspicion of tears. 'This is yet another experience I shall treasure for the rest of my life.'

CHAPTER TEN

CLAUDIA DE LEUR left Izilwane to return to East London two days after Frances had ordered her out of her house and off her property. It was Megan who had passed on this gladdening news, but Claudia's absence made no difference to the situation which had arisen between Frances and Byron. Claudia had spilled her poison, and Frances was still suffering from the effects of it.

True to his word, Byron stayed out of her way, and for three agonising weeks Frances caught only brief glimpses of him when they happened to pass each other on the road to town, and the opportunity never arose to talk to him in an attempt to straighten out their latest misunderstanding. She thought once of taking a drive to Izilwane to confront him, but pride and, she had to admit, a slight lingering doubt prevented her.

It was a frustrating and often irritating situation which was aggravated by Tony's constant, and sometimes unwanted, presence at Thorndale. He was attentive, and he was pleasant company, but he was not the man she was longing to be with.

It was May, the bushveld was still green after the late autumn rains, some of the Brahman heifers were calving, and Princess's colt was beginning to enjoy gambolling in the field with his mother. The future looked promising, and there was sufficient grazing for the cattle to last them through the mild bushveld winter, but Frances felt that a certain element of joy was missing in what she was doing.

Megan had gone to Johannesburg on a week-long visit to the publishing company which had approached her to illustrate one of their books, and Frances was missing her. The nights were lonely on the farm without Megan's warm, cheery personality, but when Tony invited her to a dance at Izilwane she was reluctant to accompany him. She felt that, under the present circumstances, Izilwane was out of bounds, but Tony's almost petulant disappointment finally made her accept his invitation.

The restaurant was filled to capacity once again that Saturday evening, but, despite the excellent quality of the food and the music, Frances could not relax. She was nervous at the thought of perhaps seeing Byron, but neither did his absence console her. It was also upsetting to notice that Tony was drinking rather heavily. He ordered one whisky after the other, and he was beginning to annoy Frances by insisting on holding her too tightly when they danced.

'Let's get some fresh air,' he suggested shortly after ten that evening, and Frances did not object.

The restaurant was beginning to feel airless, and she was hoping that the fresh air might make Tony realise he had had more than enough to drink for one evening.

It was a warm night, and they walked slowly down the path leading towards the rondawels occupied by visitors to the game park. The peace and tranquillity of the night were disturbed only by the muted sound of the music in the restaurant, and the full moon lit their path while it deepened the shadows beneath the trees.

'Frances, you like me, don't you?' Tony asked unexpectedly, turning to face her, and there was something about his lean, handsome features that disturbed her.

'Yes, of course I like you,' she answered him cautiously, knowing what would follow, and wishing there was some way she could avoid it.

'Then why won't you marry me?' he demanded with an aggression which heightened her uneasiness, but it also annoyed her.

'Oh, don't start that again, Tony!'

'No, listen,' he pleaded, stopping her with a hand on her arm when she would have turned away from him. 'Listen to me for a minute.'

'I'm listening,' she said, gritting her teeth, and forcing herself to display a tolerance which she was far from experiencing.

'We could be happy together, Frances.' He fingered the sleeves of her white blouse, and caressed her arms through the silky material, but the tremor that raced along her nerve ends was not one of pleasure. 'I promise I'll make you happy, and I'll be a good husband to you,' he pleaded in a way that made her suspect a certain instability in his behaviour that evening, and it acted as a warning to take care.

'I'm flattered that you should want to marry me, Tony, but I——' She paused abruptly, knowing that she ought to choose her words carefully, but she also knew that blunt honesty was the only thing he would understand. 'I don't love you,' she confessed.

Frances was not sure what she had expected, but the sinister look on his face frightened her, and his caressing fingers were now biting cruelly into the soft flesh of her upper arms.

'Is there someone else?'

'No, there isn't,' she lied, attempting to free her arms without aggravating the unreasonable anger which seemed to vibrate through him.

'There is! I know there is!' he hissed, a wild look in his eyes that sent a chill of fear racing through her. 'It's Rockford, isn't it? You've fallen for him!'

'Don't be silly, Tony,' she protested, forcing herself to speak quietly in the hope that it would calm him, but she knew that she had failed when Tony's lips drew back from his teeth in an ugly snarl.

'Forget him!' he advised savagely, jerking her up against him. 'I'll make you forget him!'

His hot, whisky breath was nauseating when he tried to kiss her, and her hands were against his chest in an attempt to push him away, but Tony had become instilled with a demon's strength. His mouth descended to possess hers, but she turned her head away sharply, and his warm, wet lips raked across her cheek and her throat. A wave of revulsion swept through her, and she fought him off with every ounce of strength she possessed.

'For God's sake, Tony, let me go and behave yourself!' she rebuked him sharply, hating the feel of his aroused body against her own, but her rebuke ended in a cry of pain when his hand gripped her hair to immobilise her head.

'Tell me it's *me* you want, Frances!' Tony was breathing heavily, his mouth almost touching hers, and his hips moving against hers in an attempt to arouse her, but the only thing his repulsive behaviour aroused was yet another wave of revulsion. 'Tell me!' he grated savagely when she remained silent.

'Stop that!' she cried, a terrifying darkness threatening to engulf her, and the pain in her scalp bringing tears to her eyes when she made an unsuccessful attempt to escape those rotating hips.

'Not until you tell me——' He drew a hissing breath, and his head jerked up with a furious, 'What the hell!' on his lips.

Frances was released with a staggering swiftness to see Tony dangling helplessly from a large hand which had gripped him by the jacket at the back of his neck. After her dread of meeting Byron all evening, she was suddenly so intensely relieved to see him that she wanted to burst into tears.

'Can't you take no for an answer, Phillips?' Byron queried with an ominous note in his deep voice, and his rugged features tight with an unfathomable anger when he released Tony with a slight shove that made him stagger backwards on unsteady feet.

'How dare you interfere in something that doesn't concern you!' Tony demanded furiously, breathing heavily while he shrugged his dislodged jacket into position over his shoulders. 'This happens to be between Frances and myself, so stay out of it, Rockford!'

'I don't intend to stand aside and do nothing while a woman is molested on my property,' Byron countered harshly, a hard, dangerous glitter in his eyes, and a disapproving tightness about his mouth when he glanced at Frances. 'I suggest you go inside.'

'Yes, go inside, Frances!' Tony echoed savagely, waving her away with an equally savage and threatening gesture when she bent down to pick up her evening purse, which she had dropped in the struggle. 'Perhaps Rockford and I should settle this matter between us once and for all!'

Frances did not like the look on the faces of the two men, it frightened her, and she hesitated only a moment before she said, 'I'll wait in the restaurant.'

She was shaking uncontrollably when she entered the foyer of the main building, and a wave of nausea rose inside her that sent her rushing into the ladies' room. She could not recall that she had ever felt quite so ill, as she rid her stomach of the food she had eaten that evening.

She rinsed out her mouth and applied a touch of colour to her lips, but she was still deathly pale when she finally returned to the crowded restaurant and seated herself at the table Tony had booked for them. She was outwardly composed, but her nerves were becoming frayed with tension when she looked up to see Byron skirting the dance floor and making his way among the tables towards her. Her heart raced at the sight of his tall, magnificent frame in brown slacks and brown leather jacket, and there was fortunately nothing about his appearance to indicate that he and Tony might have been involved in a physical altercation after she had left them.

'Where's Tony?' she asked, casting a nervous glance beyond Byron.

'He's left,' he answered her abruptly, his narrowed glance raking her pale face, and the muscles jutted out along the side of his strong jaw when he seated himself in the chair Tony had occupied until a little more than half an hour ago.

'And how am I supposed to get home?' she asked with a mixture of dismay and relief.

'I'll take you,' he said, 'but only after you've danced one dance with me.'

'And if I refuse?' she questioned him warily, not quite sure how she ought to have reacted to his statement, and convinced that he had sensed her uncertainty when she saw him raise a slightly amused eyebrow.

'It's a long walk to Thorndale.'

'That's blackmail!' she protested indignantly, feeling as if she had escaped the dishonourable intentions of one man only to find herself at the mercy of another whose intentions were not yet quite clear to her.

'Take it or leave it,' Byron shrugged with a carelessness that had the power to hurt her, and her hand rose to her throat to still that throbbing, aching pulse.

'I'll take it,' she said, her voice unnaturally husky with the effort to speak.

'Sensible choice,' he agreed, a laconic smile curving his mouth as he reached across the small table to take her hand and draw her to her feet.

They swayed together to the slow beat of the music provided by the local three-piece band, but it was a bittersweet sensation to be so close to him and yet so far removed from the heart of the man. He was frowning and glancing at his watch from time to time as if he was wishing this dance would end so that he could take her home, and she wondered miserably why he had bothered to ask her to dance with him when it so obviously pained him to do so.

'You're not really enjoying this dance, are you?' she said when she could no longer bear his cool aloofness while everything inside her cried out with a longing so intense that she wanted to weep, and his reaction to her statement was even more painful.

'Let's go,' he said curtly, taking her arm and ushering her off the floor.

They left the restaurant when Frances had collected her evening purse at the table, and walked in silence along the flagstone path to where Byron had parked his Land Rover beside his bungalow, as with difficulty she curbed the ridiculous tears which threatened to spill from her lashes.

She was sitting stiffly beside him in the Land Rover while he inserted the key in the ignition, and she expected to hear the engine turning over, but instead she heard an angry exclamation spilling from Byron's lips which made her heart leap nervously in her breast when he turned abruptly in his seat to face her.

'Frances!' There was a strange urgency in his deep voice when he spoke her name, and she felt the breath still in her throat. 'I think I know who's been cutting the fence between our properties, and I have a strong suspicion that we might catch the culprit tonight.'

'*What?*' she demanded incredulously, blinking back her tears, and not quite sure that she had heard him correctly.

'I want to be waiting there for him tonight, and I'd like you to come with me,' Byron added with that strange urgency which still lingered in the gravelly depths of his voice.

'I'll come with you, but——' She stared intently at his rugged face, trying to read his expression in the darkened interior of the Land Rover, and failing. 'May I know whom you suspect?'

'Tony Phillips.'

Frances knew that she could not have been more stunned if a bomb had suddenly exploded in her lap. Her mouth was gaping, and she lifted her sagging jaw hastily when she came to her senses.

'*Tony?* You suspect *Tony?*' she almost shrieked at Byron. 'You must be out of your mind!'

'We shall see,' he said abruptly, turning the key in the

ignition, and driving away from his bungalow towards the exit of the camp.

Frances lapsed into a troubled and disbelieving silence while they drove slowly through the park to where the river camp adjoined the game park. Her mind was spinning with the effort of her relentless search for something which would make Byron's accusation credible, but she had found nothing by the time Byron eased the nose of his Land Rover into the deep shadows of the acacia trees and pointed it directly at the fence which was about fifteen metres away.

He switched off the engine as well as the lights, and they sat for some time listening to the sound of the crickets in the undergrowth and the mournful howl of a jackal. The lion roared once, twice in the distance, and then he, too, fell silent.

'Byron, you can't be serious about suspecting Tony?' Frances broke the silence between them when she could no longer tolerate the incredible strain of not knowing.

'I *am* serious.'

'But he's so—so——'

'Sweet and harmless?' he filled in for her with a hint of cynical amusement in his lowered voice, and she felt an embarrassing warmth invading her cheeks which she was glad he could not see.

'Well . . . yes . . . in a way,' she heard herself admitting haltingly. 'And I'm not counting his behaviour this evening,' she added with a self-conscious laugh.

Byron was silent for a moment, and she turned her head to look at him, but it was too dark beneath the trees to see his face.

'Tony Phillips is not the sweet, harmless man you imagine him to be, Frances,' he said at length. 'Heavy drinking, high living, and excessive gambling have left him with his farm heavily mortgaged and his creditors demanding payment. He held them off at first with promises of repayment when he inherited Thorndale, but George Wilkins was not a fool. He knew about his nephew wasting away his inheritance, and he made very sure that the same thing was not going to happen to Thorndale after his death.'

Frances was shocked by this disclosure. She did not doubt that Byron had spoken the truth, but she was finding it difficult to accept when she had believed almost the opposite of Tony.

'So that's why Tony didn't inherit the farm,' she murmured, finding the answer at last to something which had puzzled her for some time. 'But that still doesn't explain why you suspect him of cutting the fence,' she persisted with her probing.

'I've suspected him for some time, but I'm not going to give you my reasons at the moment.' Byron's voice was a low and angry rumble when he answered her. 'What I will tell you is this. Phillips was in a dangerous mood when he left the camp this evening, and my suspicions were strengthened by a certain careless remark he passed. He said that before this night ended I would be made to regret that I intruded on something which didn't concern me.'

'Dear heaven!' She expelled the air from her lungs without realising that she had held her breath. 'Is it possible that you can think you know someone, and then find you don't know them at all?'

'It's possible.'

His terse reply struck a discomfiting chord inside her, and she had difficulty in shrugging it off.

'If your suspicions are correct ... how long do you think we might have to wait?'

'I'm not sure.' The leather of his jacket creaked against the seat as he shifted himself into a more comfortable position behind the wheel. 'I'm not even absolutely sure that anything will happen this evening, but I have to act on this feeling that it might.'

Frances did not respond to that remark. She could understand his feelings, but she could not help wishing he would be wrong about Tony, and she was afraid of what she knew she might see.

The minutes must have stretched into an hour while they sat without speaking in the darkness. They were both staring into the river camp beyond the fence where they could see the white blur of some of her Brahman cattle in the moonlight, and nothing stirred except the shadows which were starting to dance in front of her tired eyes.

'It's getting late,' she said eventually, stifling a yawn behind her fingers, and blinking the moisture from her eyes.

'I know, and I'm beginning to regret that I dragged you out here for nothing when——' Byron broke off abruptly, and she could almost feel his body stiffen beside her in the darkness of the Land Rover.

'What is it?' she asked, her heart beating nervously in the region of her throat.

'Quiet!' he muttered sharply.

Frances strained her ears for a sound, *any* sound, and then she heard it. 'I can hear a horse approaching.'

'Yes,' he whispered back hissingly. 'Our long wait hasn't been in vain after all.'

Frances could feel her insides start to shake while they waited for the horseman to come into sight, and a few seconds later they saw him riding at a slow trot towards the fence. He dismounted, leaving his horse untethered, and she felt a shiver racing along her spine during the ensuing silence while he stood like a statue in the moonlight. He was wearing a hat which was pulled down over his eyes to leave his face in deep shadow, and Frances could scarcely breathe while she watched and waited, not wanting to believe, but when he raised a hand to rub the back of his neck in a quick, all too familiar gesture, she *knew*.

'Dear God, it—it *is* Tony!' she stammered with a smothered gasp, and was aware of Byron quietly opening the door. 'What are you planning to do?' she whispered anxiously, her heart thudding against her breastbone.

'I'm going to wait until he's actually cut the fence, and then I'm going to nab him,' Byron explained quietly, leaning towards her until his mouth was close to her ear. 'Now, listen carefully. I'm going to get as close to the fence as I can without being seen, but I want you to switch on the searchlight and turn it on him the minute you hear me call out to him. Got that?'

She nodded, and then, realising he could not see her clearly in the darkness of the vehicle, she whispered, 'Yes.'

'Good girl!' he replied, his heavy hand squeezing her shoulder briefly before he moved away from her.

'Byron!' She reached out anxiously, clutching at the sleeve of his leather jacket as fear, like a cold, clammy hand, gripped her insides. 'Be careful!'

His warm hand closed briefly and comfortingly over hers before he loosened the clasp of her fingers and got out quietly to blend swiftly with shadows which had suddenly adopted a sinister appearance.

Frances wiped her clammy hands against the folds of her black skirt, and she could feel them trembling when she fingered the controls of the searchlight in readiness for the signal Byron would give her, but her glance was riveted to the shadowy figure now kneeling directly beyond the fence. The rhythmic snap of the wire cutters was faint, but it jarred her nerves, making her flinch, and she could imagine the strong wire fence curling aside with each snip to leave a gaping opening which was growing larger every second.

'You're not going to get away with it this time, Phillips!'

Byron's raised, angry voice was the signal she had waited for, and her trembling fingers activated the searchlight, turning it full on Tony. He flung up an arm to shield his face, stooping at the same time to pick up something, and Frances leaned forward, staring in horror when she realised he had a rifle in his hands.

The events that followed happened with such incredible speed that she could scarcely believe it afterwards. For one fraction of a terrifying second she was still thinking, '*God, he's going to kill Byron!*', and the next there was an explosion that slammed her back against her seat while it left the windscreen looking like a frosted web. A second shot followed rapidly on the first to shatter the glass casing of the searchlight, and everything was plunged into darkness.

'*Damn* you, you blasted fool!' she heard Byron shout, while she sat staring stupidly into the blackness which her eyes needed time to adjust to, and it was at this point that she felt a numb, burning pain in her left shoulder.

She raised her hand to it, and the damp warmth seeping into her blouse startled her. It was blood. *Her* blood. And her eyes widened with incredulity and a touch of fear. She had been shot!

Her senses sharpened to an unfamiliar pitch. She heard Tony galloping away on horseback under cover of the ensuing darkness, and then there were running footsteps approaching the vehicle. The door was jerked open violently on her side, and the interior light was switched on.

'My God!' Byron exclaimed, ashen-faced, and she followed the direction of his gaze to see the dark red stain spreading against the white silk of her long-sleeved blouse. 'My God!' he said again, taking off his leather jacket and flinging it across her on to the driver's seat. 'Phillips is going to pay for this!'

Frances was momentarily too shocked to speak while she watched him take off his white shirt and tear it into long strips. The pain was increasing in her shoulder as the numbness receded, and she had to grit her teeth not to cry out.

'Frances?' Byron framed her white face in his hands, and there was anxiety in his tawny glance when he looked into her pain-filled eyes. 'I have to try and stem the flow of blood, so don't pass out on me just yet.'

'I'm not the fainting type,' she said through her teeth, trying to smile up at him despite the near intolerable pain she was having to endure. 'Do whatever you have to do.'

'I'll try not to hurt you,' he said thickly, unbuttoning her blouse carefully and sliding it gently aside to expose her shoulder and the curve of her breast in the flimsy lacy bra.

This was not the time to feel embarrassed, but her cheekbones felt as if they were on fire, and Byron's rugged features looked so grim and white in the dim interior of the Land Rover that she tried to make light of the situation.

'Have you—had a lot of practice with—this sort of thing?' she asked him, fighting against the pain when he lifted the strap of her bra and slid it aside to examine her shoulder.

'I've seen a couple of wounds in my time,' he answered her grimly, and an amused smile plucked at her lips.

'I was—referring to your—expertise in—undressing women,' she explained, sinking her teeth into her lower lip when he rolled a portion of his shirt into a wad and pressed it against her shoulder to stem the flow of blood which was trickling down along her breast to stain her bra, and she saw his tightly compressed mouth twitch with a hint of a smile.

'I've had a fair amount of practice in that field as well.'

'That's to be—expected I—suppose,' she murmured haltingly, trying to cope with the excruciating pain in her shoulder as well as an added stab of jealousy, but the latter was forgotten when she heard him draw a sharp breath while his fingers gently probed her shoulder blade. 'What's wrong?'

'The bullet has lodged in your shoulder,' Byron explained in an oddly clipped voice. 'I'm going to have to get you to hospital as quickly as possible.'

'Are you sure?'

'I'm sure,' he nodded, placing her hand against the wad of material to hold it there while he took the long strips he had torn off his shirt, and used them as a bandage.

'Oh, dear!' she groaned, a lightheadedness assailing her, and tremors erupting inside her that made her shake uncontrollably as if she was freezing. 'This is going to—to scare the daylights out—out of Dad and—and Olivia.'

'It can't be helped,' he answered her brusquely, tightening the knot on his improvised bandage.

'Byron!' she gasped, a new fear surging through her when she felt herself losing her battle against the pain and that terrible blackness which was threatening to engulf her. 'I—I'm not going to—to die, am I?'

'Not if I can help it!' he assured her in a harsh, oddly grating voice, and his ashen face seemed to go a shade paler when he reached over her for his leather jacket to drape it about her for added warmth.

'That's good because I——' Frances broke off abruptly, her teeth chattering with the cold and making it awkward to speak. She did not want to die before she had had time to apologise, and time to tell him how much she loved him, but she could say none of these things as she stared up at Byron through a film of gathering mist which was distorting his features and making his face come and go in rapid succession. 'You look so—funny and so far—away.'

Her head lolled back against the seat, it was suddenly too heavy to hold up, and then someone put out the light.

Frances came to her senses on a trolley which was being pushed along a corridor in the hospital, and Dr Jessica Neal and her uncle, Dr Peter O'Brien, were walking on either side of her.

'Hello, what's happening?' she asked, aware of the pain, but no longer finding it unbearable.

'You're going into the theatre,' her uncle explained the reason for their green theatre gowns with a tight smile about his mouth. 'Jessica's going to operate, and I'm going to assist.'

'And you're going to be all right,' Jessica Neal added with a reassuring smile to which Frances responded weakly before a look of anxiety entered her eyes.

'Dad and Olivia?' she asked.

'They're here.' Her uncle's lean face creased into a smile for the first time. 'And so is your aunt.'

That's good, Frances thought hazily. Aunty Viv is at her best in a crisis, and Dad and Olivia will need her with them in this particular crisis.

'And Byron?' she whispered her query anxiously.

'Wild horses, apparently, wouldn't get him away from this hospital,' Jessica Neal answered with a teasing light in her dark brown eyes as they wheeled the trolley into the antiseptic-smelling theatre, and Frances sighed tiredly, knowing that she was in good hands, and allowing herself to drift into that twilight world where nothing mattered.

Frances was emerging from a second bout of blackness, and she drifted for some time in a misty, distorted tunnel with Byron's voice drawing her towards that dim light which she could see up ahead. She must be dreaming that he was sitting there beside her bed, but the hand holding hers was very real, and he was saying something which was too incredible to imagine could be anything but part of a dream.

'I love you, and you've got to believe me.'

Her fingers tightened instinctively about his, and she turned her head on the pillow, opening her eyes slowly to find him sitting beside her bed with a haggard, drawn look on his face, and a stubble of beard darkening his strong jaw.

'What . . . did you say?' she asked, her voice a weak whisper, and he pushed his fingers in an uncharacteristic gesture through his dark hair to make it fall back untidily across his broad forehead.

'I asked how you were feeling,' he said, and a slight frown creased her smooth brow.

Was it possible that she could have heard him

incorrectly, or had it simply been part of an awakening dream? Was she so desperate to hear him say that he loved her, that she could have conjured it up in her own mind?

'I'm fine, I——' She tried to sit up in her agitation, but the stabbing pain in her shoulder was a reminder of why she was in hospital, and she winced as she sagged back against the pillows with her dark hair spilling across the white starched linen.

'Lie still,' Byron warned unnecessarily, his rugged features forbidding as he leaned forward to lift a heavy strand of hair away from her throat and her injured shoulder.

'I don't appear to be in a fit state to do anything else at the moment,' she sighed tiredly, closing her eyes for a moment. 'What time is it?'

'Four-thirty.'

'In the morning?' Her dark lashes lifted in surprise, and she stared at Byron incredulously, knowing the answer to her next query even before she asked it. 'Have you been here all night?'

'Yes.'

'Oh, Byron!' she whispered, her fingers tightening about his as she probed his glance in the hope of finding the reason for his unnatural concern, but his tired eyes were shuttered. 'Where's everyone else?' she asked at length, turning her face away from him when she realised that she was perilously close to tears.

'They saw you when you came out of the theatre, and they spoke to you.' Her blank expression when she turned her face to his again made him raise a questioning eyebrow. 'Don't you remember?'

'No,' she whispered, frowning in her attempt to remember, and praying that she had not said anything which might have been too revealing.

'Well, anyway, I told them to go home, and I promised I'd give them a call the moment you were awake, which is what I'm going to do now.'

'Byron . . .' Her fingers tightened almost convulsively about his, preventing him from leaving when he rose from the chair beside her high hospital bed, and she looked up at him anxiously. 'What's going to happen to Tony?'

Byron's mouth tightened, and the muscles jutted out angrily along the sides of his unshaven jaw. 'The matter is now in the hands of the police.'

'He didn't mean to shoot me,' she murmured defensively, and with a certain amount of pity. 'I'm sure he didn't even know I was there, and they're not going to arrest him for that. Are they?'

'I hope they do,' said Byron in that low, angry growl that reminded her of the rumble of thunder. 'It's also a felony to go about cutting fences between people's properties, especially if that fence happens to surround a game park, and whether we like it or not Tony Phillips is not going to get off lightly on either score.'

That was true, she supposed. Tony would have to be brought to justice, and there was really nothing they could do about it now the police were involved.

'Byron . . .' Frances clung tightly to his hand when he would have removed it from hers, and her eyes filled with those tears she could no longer suppress. 'Thanks for— for everything.'

She could not see his expression through the blur of her embarrassing tears, but he raised her hand, and she felt his beard scraping against her fingers when he pressed his lips unexpectedly to her knuckles.

'Rest now, and get better,' he said in a throaty, unfamiliar voice as he lowered her hand to the sheets and moved away from the bed. 'I'm going to tell the Sister you're awake, and then I'm going to give your folks a call at Mountain View.'

She did not see him leave, she had closed her eyes to stem the flow of tears, but she heard his heavy footsteps leave her ward and disappear down the passage, and her heart felt like a piece of lead in her breast.

CHAPTER ELEVEN

FRANCES was released from hospital a few days later, but she had seldom been without visitors, and her room had been filled daily with fresh flowers from Olivia's garden as well as her aunt's. Byron had presented her with a basket of fruit, and it brought a smile to her lips to recall how awkward he had looked at the time. He had visited her regularly every evening, but he had never stayed long, and they had never been alone to clear up the terrible misunderstanding between them.

No one questioned her about that night when she had been accidentally shot. Frances knew that Byron would have told her family everything they might have wanted to know, and she was grateful that the subject was avoided when they came to visit her. She did not want to talk about what had happened. It was depressing to recall how she had misjudged Tony, and it was too upsetting to remember that terrifying moment when she had thought that Byron might be killed. Afterwards she had been afraid that she might die before she had had an opportunity to tell Byron how much she . . .! Oh, what was the sense of it? She had seen him every day, but not once had he displayed anything more than polite concern, and that was all he would ever feel for her. Polite concern! Oh, God, how was she going to bear it?

Frances was not allowed to return to Thorndale when she was released from hospital. Olivia insisted that she spend a few days at Mountain View to recuperate, and the rest of the family agreed. Dr Jessica Neal was also supportive of Olivia's decision.

'You'll need a few days to regain your strength,' she warned Frances the morning she was released from hospital, 'and don't attempt to do anything too strenuous at first. That wound will need time to heal properly, and it will be a while before you regain the full use of your arm.'

Frances was having tea with Olivia and her Aunt Vivien on Mountain View's sunny, gauzed-in verandah when she realised that Dr Jessica Neal had spoken the truth. She had been out of hospital for almost a week, and she felt healthy and strong in every other respect, but the stiffness in her left arm had persisted, and made it difficult for her to perform the most menial tasks without a certain amount of discomfort.

'I know it's frustrating, pet, but don't rush it,' Aunty Viv warned when she saw Frances flexing her fingers and clenching her fist experimentally. 'You've worked very hard for some years now without a decent break, so relax and think of this as a holiday, even if it is enforced.'

'I agree with your aunt, darling,' Olivia smiled, and she was about to add something when the sound of an approaching car made her glance quickly in the direction of the road leading up to the house. 'It looks as if we have a visitor,' she murmured, frowning.

'It's Tony Phillips,' Frances enlightened Olivia when she recognised the red BMW.

'That young man has a nerve coming here after what he did!' Vivien O'Brien exploded, her dark eyes filling with anger as she rose to her feet.

'Shall I tell him to leave, Frances?' asked Olivia, her grey glance mirroring her concern when she noticed the paleness which had settled in Frances' cheeks.

'No,' she answered Olivia quietly. 'Let him come in.'

There were certain things she had to know, and Tony was the only one who could give her the answers she required. She saw him get out of his car and hesitate a moment with an unfamiliar uncertainty before he walked towards the house and opened the gauze door on to the verandah where Frances remained seated, while Aunty Viv and Olivia confronted him with an angry, silent stance.

'Good morning,' Tony greeted them with a lack of his usual boldness, and their distant response made him shift about uncomfortably on his feet when he directed his gaze at Frances. 'I won't take up much of your time, Frances, but I was released on bail this morning, and I have to talk to you.'

She nodded and cast a quick glance at Olivia and her aunt. 'Would you leave us alone for a few minutes, please?'

Aunty Viv's brown eyes flashed with wariness and anger when she looked at Tony. 'Well, I——'

'We'll be in the lounge if you need us,' Olivia interrupted her sister-in-law hastily and, taking Vivien's arm, she entered the house to leave Frances and Tony alone on the verandah.

Frances gestured him into a chair, and he seated himself, staring down at his hands for some time before he spoke.

'I'm sorry about what happened, Frances,' he said with a genuine look of regret on his lean, handsome face. 'I swear I never knew you were in the Land Rover when I fired at the searchlight.'

'I realised that.' The memory of that night was like a nightmare, and she cast it aside hurriedly. 'Why did you do it, Tony? What did you hope to gain by cutting the fence between Thorndale and Izilwane?'

'I was desperate, Frances, and that's the truth,' he answered her with a surprising honesty despite the dull redness that seeped into his tanned cheeks. 'You were my only hope when I didn't inherit Thorndale, and marrying you would have helped to ease me out of my financial predicament. I knew that your relationship with Rockford was rather sticky at first and, for my own sake, I was determined to keep it that way. I watched you closely, and when both you and Rockford showed periodic signs of settling the differences between you I would cut the fence between your properties in the hope of aggravating the friction between you.'

Frances had no idea what she had expected to hear, but his confession left her speechless for several seconds until a wave of anger loosened her tongue. 'For God's sake, Tony, how could you have been so—so——'

'I know,' he interrupted her when she was still searching for the right word to express her feelings, and he had the grace to look ashamed. 'I know what you must think of me, and I don't blame you. I also admit that I went a little crazy the other night, but I was mad with jealousy. You see, Frances, the craziest thing of all is that I actually fell in love with you, and I lost my head the other night when I realised that I didn't stand a chance against Byron Rockford.'

This came as an even greater shock to her, and she stared at him helplessly. 'I don't know what to say to you.'

'There's no need to say anything,' he assured her, smiling twistedly. 'I'll take whatever punishment is coming my way, but that doesn't exactly solve my problems, so I shall have to sell The Grove to pay my long-overdue debts—and that's another reason why I came to see you.' He lowered his gaze self-consciously to his hands and shifted awkwardly on his chair. 'I don't think Rockford would treat me very kindly if I had to go and see him now, but I'd like you to give him a message from me. Tell him I'm selling The Grove and, if he's interested, I'd like to give him first option to buy the farm.'

Frances felt her heart lurch with a wild hope, but her face remained expressionless. 'I'll tell him.'

'Well, that's it, then,' he said, the cane chair creaking beneath him when he got to his feet. 'I don't think we'll see each other again, so this has to be goodbye, and I can only hope that you'll forgive me in time.'

He held out his hand, and Frances slowly placed hers in it. 'Goodbye, Tony.'

She could not help feeling sorry for him after he had gone. He had looked rather pathetic, but, as everyone would be quick to remind her, he had only himself to blame for the unfortunate position he now found himself in.

Byron arrived at Mountain View that afternoon in time to have tea with Frances and Olivia, but Frances did not mention Tony's visit that morning until she had a moment alone with Byron.

'Tony is out on bail, and he came to see me this morning,' she said without preamble when Olivia went inside for a few minutes, and Byron's rugged features hardened.

'What did he want?'

'He came to apologise and to say goodbye,' she explained, turning slightly to face the khaki-clad man seated on the bench beside her. 'He also asked me to tell you that he's selling The Grove, and he'd like you to have first option to buy.' The expression on Byron's rugged features did not alter, and she found it difficult to gauge his feelings on this matter. 'Are you interested?'

'I might be,' he said abruptly, reaching down on to the floor beside him to pick up the flat box he had placed there on his arrival. 'I have something here for you.'

'For me?' she asked in astonishment when the neatly wrapped box was placed in her lap. 'What is it?'

'Why don't you open it and see for yourself?'

She did as she was told, her fingers trembling slightly when she removed the wrapping and lifted the lid. She brushed aside the tissue paper and, to her dismay, found a white silk blouse very similar to the one which had been ruined that night when she had collected a bullet in her shoulder.

'Oh, Byron, you shouldn't have!' she protested, her voice a mixture of pleasure and dismay as she fingered the expensive silk.

'I owe it to you,' he said tersely. 'If I'd had any sense I wouldn't have taken you with me that night, and then you wouldn't be sitting here recovering from a gunshot wound which might easily have killed you. I blame myself for this entirely.'

'Oh, Byron, I wish you wouldn't say that,' Frances protested once again. 'No one, least of all you, could have foreseen what would happen that night.'

Byron's features remained granite-hard with self-condemnation. 'I saw what mood he was in when he left the camp, and I should have anticipated his actions.'

'Oh, well, how wonderful if we could always anticipate the actions of others,' she mocked him gently, 'but how dull the world would be without all those unexpected surprises which so often make life worth living.'

Byron's intent, narrowed gaze was slightly unnerving, but his sensuous mouth finally curved in a smile which seemed to melt her bones. 'I guess you're right in a way.'

His compelling glance held hers, and she felt flustered when she finally managed to drag her eyes away from his.

'Thank you, Byron,' she murmured and, when he made a gesture as if he did not understand, she added hastily, 'for the blouse, I mean.'

'Don't I deserve a kiss along with the "thank you"?' he mocked her, and she felt that embarrassing warmth steel into her cheeks.

'You do, if that's what you want,' she said, clinging to the fragments of her composure as she leaned towards him to kiss his cheek, but he turned his head at the last moment, and their lips met while his hand at the nape of her neck prevented her from pulling away when she would have done so.

His hard mouth moved against hers, parting her lips with a warm, gentle sensuality, and an exhilarating fire raced along her veins that left her trembling inwardly when he finally released her. This was the first time he had kissed her since that morning when he had walked out of her study after announcing that he wanted to marry her, and she wondered if he was remembering that as well.

'How did you know this blouse would be the right

size?' She said the first thing that entered her mind in her attempt to ease the situation on to a comfortable level.

'I told Megan what I wanted, and asked her to buy it for me.' He glanced at his watch, and got to his feet. 'I'm afraid I have to go now.'

Frances set aside the gift he had brought her, and rose with him. 'Will I see you again tomorrow?'

Dear heaven! How she hated herself for being so obvious, and his shuttered expression made her feel a thousand times worse.

'If I'm not too busy.'

'Of course,' she replied hastily and, gesturing to the box she had left on the bench, she added, 'thank you once again.'

'You're welcome,' he brushed the matter aside with a wave of his hand, and then he was striding away from the house to where he had parked his dusty Land Rover.

Frances was miserable after Byron had left, and she felt worse when he stayed away the following day. He telephoned two days later, but she was not at home that morning. She had been driving round the farm with her father in his open jeep, and it was only when they returned home for lunch that Olivia passed on Byron's message.

'Byron said he'd be calling for you at four-thirty this afternoon, and he told me not to expect you home for dinner.' There was a hint of mischief in Olivia's grey eyes. 'I didn't get the idea that he was issuing an invitation, it sounded very much like an order, and he had a very determined note in his voice.'

'Hmf!' Bernard King grunted when they sat down to lunch. 'A man will never get anywhere with a woman by issuing those polite invitations.'

'Who says he wants to get anywhere with me?' Frances demanded indignantly, and her father raised his eyebrows in mock surprise.

'Who says he doesn't?'

'Now what kind of an answer is that?' she wanted to

know, sighing exasperatedly, and refusing to build up her hopes when she was convinced that she had nothing to hope for.

'What kind of an answer did you expect?' her father countered with a hint of teasing mockery in his dark eyes. 'Be ready when he calls for you this afternoon, and play it by ear from there.'

Play it by ear? If she played it by ear she would make a hopeless idiot of herself by showing Byron exactly how much she cared, and that was the last thing on earth she wanted to do.

Frances chose to wear a grey skirt with the white blouse which Byron had given her, and she was not going to deny to herself that her choice had been influenced by a desire to please him. The nights could be cool during the winter months, and the blouse also hid the tender scar on her shoulder. She looked tanned and healthy with her long hair tied back with her favourite blue scarf, but her left arm was still stiff and lazy in its responses.

Byron arrived at Mountain View at precisely four-thirty, and his black slacks and shirt added a dangerous and devilish look to his ruggedly handsome appearance. His tawny glance flicked over her, noting the fact that she was wearing his gift, and a tiny smile curved his mouth when he helped her into the Land Rover.

'Where are we going?' she asked curiously when they were leaving Mountain View.

'You'll find out soon enough,' was the only answer Frances received, and she lapsed into an uneasy silence.

They could only be going to Izilwane, she realised afterwards when he took the road in that direction, but she wondered why he was being so mysterious about it. It was time she returned to her farm, she decided when they passed the entrance to Thorndale. She had also inconvenienced Megan long enough. The twenty-minute trip twice daily between Louisville and Izilwane was tiring, but Megan had had no option but to stay with her parents while Frances was away from Thorndale.

The sun was beginning to set when Byron drove at a leisurely pace through the game park, and monkeys were chattering and leaping from one branch to another in trees which were casting long shadows across the veld.

'We discovered yesterday that the lioness is in whelp,' Byron informed her, slowing down and stopping the vehicle when a herd of impala leapt across the road with that graceful agility they possessed.

'I'm so glad,' she replied, and she meant it sincerely, but Byron glanced at her sharply as if he did not believe her entirely. 'I *am* glad for your sake,' she repeated firmly, and he left the matter there as he drove on.

The water in the large dam lay blinking ahead of them in the late afternoon sun and, as Byron parked his Land Rover at the entrance to the pier where the launch was moored, Frances was forced to recall the previous occasion when he had taken her out on the launch.

'Do I have to carry you again, or do you come peaceably this time?' he smiled at her, and her cheeks went pink.

'I'll come peaceably,' she promised, getting out of the Land Rover and walking with him on to the wooden pier.

Byron helped her on to the launch, making sure that she was seated comfortably before he turned to the controls, and a few moments later the engines were throbbing into the late afternoon silence as he steered the launch towards the centre of the dam.

'This is the best time of the day to go out on the launch,' he explained. 'The bushveld sunsets are beautiful, as you must know, and one can watch the animals coming down to the water to drink.'

Frances felt tense and uneasy for some inexplicable reason, and she sat in silence while she watched the setting sun descend slowly like a red ball of fire in the sky. Two hadedas swooped low overhead, their ha-ha-ha-dahah call shattering the silence after Byron had cut the engines of the launch a reasonable distance from the water's edge, and Frances rose with a sigh to lean against the rail.

'Look, there's a herd of zebra and wildebeest,' she said, pointing when Byron joined her at the rail, and they stood observing the animals in silence while the sun dipped lower to add a touch of pink and gold to the fleecy clouds in the sky. She turned to Byron at last, incapable of bearing the tension between them a moment longer. 'Why did you bring me here?'

His sensuous mouth twitched with the suggestion of a smile. 'I thought we could watch the sunset together, and I thought it was the ideal place for what I have to tell you.'

Her heart lurched in something close to fear, and she went strangely cold. 'What is it that you have to tell me?'

'I've made Phillips an offer for The Grove through Thomas Atherstone, and he's accepted it.'

Frances had no idea what she had imagined he would have to tell her, but this was not quite what she had expected, and neither did it ease that unbearable tension inside her.

'Congratulations,' she said stiffly. 'Now you can extend Izilwane to your heart's content.'

'That isn't quite what I have in mind,' Byron smiled into the gathering dusk. 'I'll use a portion of the land to extend the game park, but I'd like to try my hand at cattle ranching on the remainder, and that's where you come in.'

'I can't see how your decision affects me,' she said, raising her startled eyes to his, and his smile deepened.

'I can only make a success of it if you'll agree to help me with your expert knowledge.'

'I thought farming wasn't a woman's job,' she remarked, unable to resist this opportunity to deliver that jab, and his smile became twisted with self-mockery as he turned slightly to face her.

'You've proved me wrong in your case, but I still

maintain that farming isn't a job which most women would cope with successfully.'

Frances regarded him in silence, not quite sure whether she ought to be pleased or angry, then she inclined her head slightly in acknowledgement. 'Thank you for that.'

He lifted her hand off the rail, his touch unbearably sweet, and her wary heart leapt wildly in her breast when he raised it to his lips in the same way he had done in the hospital.

'Perhaps you'll believe now that I'm not out to get my hands on Thorndale if I ask you to marry me.' She was speechless with wonder as she stared up at him, almost too afraid to believe what she saw in his eyes. This, then, was what Olivia had meant when she had said that it would be an experience which would remain with her for the rest of her life when Byron allowed her to see into his heart. Everything she had longed for was there for her to see, and she would be a fool not to believe it. 'Frances, I love you more than I could ever tell you,' he added, his fingers tightening almost painfully about hers in his anxiety, 'and you've got to believe me, or I swear to you I'll dog your footsteps day and night until you do!'

'I *did* hear you say you loved me when I was coming round after the operation,' she accused, her eyes glowing unnaturally bright as if with a fever when she realised the truth. 'I did hear you say it, didn't I?'

'Yes,' he murmured, smiling against her fingers.

'But why wouldn't you repeat it when I asked you to?'

'I was afraid you wouldn't believe me.'

That made sense, painful sense, and she swayed towards him, leaning her head against his shoulder when she felt her eyes stinging.

'Oh, Byron!' she sighed, letting the misery flow from her at last with the tears that spilled from her lashes. 'I owe you an apology.'

'No,' he said, tilting her face up to his to kiss away her tears, and taking her gently into his arms so that her body could rest against his. 'My timing was out completely, and your remarks were quite justifiable under the circumstances.'

'What made Claudia do it?'

'She was trying out her fancy wiles on me after you left the tearoom that morning, and I put her in her place by telling her there was someone else,' he explained with a grimace. 'It didn't take much effort for her to guess that it was you, and she didn't pass up the opportunity of spilling some of her venom.'

'I thought you liked her.'

'Don't be ridiculous!' he rebuked her with a deep-throated laugh before he lowered his head and brushed his lips lightly against hers. 'It amused me to see the two of you together. It was like putting a real diamond next to an imitation and, no matter what Claudia did, she could never outshine you.'

'I'm glad she's gone,' she sighed, finding it difficult to read his expression in the darkness which had settled like a protective blanket over the bushveld.

'So am I,' Byron agreed with her, then he held her away from him with a hint of exasperation in his manner. 'Frances, how much longer are you going to make me wait for an answer?'

Didn't he know? Hadn't he guessed? Was it possible that he could have been as blind as she? She raised her hands, exploring the rugged contours of his face with her fingers as she had longed to do, and she did not delay telling him what she knew he was waiting to hear.

'I love you . . . desperately . . . and yes, I'll marry you,' she said, her voice choked with emotion, and she felt a tremor in the hands that drew her towards him.

'Darling,' he groaned into her hair. 'My darling girl!'

'Hold me close, Byron,' she pleaded, his gentleness unbearably sweet, but she needed so much more than that. 'Hold me tightly, and tell me again that you love me.'

'I don't want to hurt your shoulder,' he gruffly

explained the reason for his peculiar restraint.

'Forget about my shoulder! Hold me and tell me again that you love me!' she pleaded almost desperately.

'I love you,' he groaned, and this time he crushed her against him with a satisfying force which almost drove the breath from her body as he set his mouth on hers and kissed her with a fiery passion that left her limp and trembling in his arms.

His mouth explored her face and her throat with sensual, tantalising kisses while his hands stroked her body, arousing her to an aching need which was like a liquid fire surging through her veins to reach every vital part of her anatomy. The buttons of her blouse gave way beneath his fingers, and he brushed the silky material aside to press his lips to the neat little scar against her shoulder while his fingers slid beneath the lace at her breast to stroke the rounded flesh and probe the hardened peak. The intimacy of those stroking fingers heightened her desire, and she clung to him with a moan of pleasure on her lips as she yielded against his equally aroused body with an eagerness she no longer had the need to be ashamed of.

'God, Frances!' he murmured, his deep voice vibrant with the extent of his emotions when he released her and held her a little away from him. 'I love you, and I want you, but I think it's time I got this launch back to the pier. I've ordered a special dinner for us at the restaurant, and we have to decide on a suitable wedding date, but, I'm warning you, it had better be soon!'

'Oh, Byron . . . darling . . . I love you so much,' she whispered ecstatically, melting into arms which were only too eager to hold her, and several more seconds elapsed before Byron started the engines to return the launch to the pier.

Frances sighed contentedly into the darkness when she stood at the controls with Byron's arm firmly about her, and her head resting comfortably against his shoulder. The sun had set, but there would be other sunsets at Izilwane, and she would cherish each one of them.

Harlequin Presents

Coming Next Month

Available in November wherever paperback books are sold, or through Harlequin Reader Service:

In the U.S.
901 Fuhrmann Blvd.
P.O. Box 1397
Buffalo, N.Y. 14240-1397

In Canada
P.O. Box 603
Fort Erie, Ontario
L2A 5X3

What the press says about Harlequin romance fiction...

"When it comes to romantic novels...
Harlequin is the indisputable king."
—*New York Times*

"...always with an upbeat, happy ending."
—*San Francisco Chronicle*

"Women have come to trust these
stories about contemporary people,
set in exciting foreign places."
—*Best Sellers*, New York

"The most popular reading matter of
American women today."
— *Detroit News*

"...a work of art."
— *Globe & Mail*, Toronto

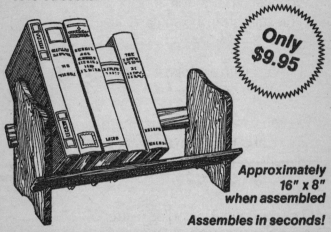

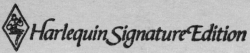

Harlequin Signature Edition

Penny Jordan

Stronger Than Yearning

He was the man of her dreams!

The same dark hair, the same mocking eyes; it was as if the
Regency rake of the portrait, the seducer of Jenna's dream, had
come to life. Jenna, believing the last of the Deverils dead, was
determined to buy the great old Yorkshire Hall—to claim it for
her daughter, Lucy, and put to rest some of the painful memories of Lucy's birth. She had no way of knowing that a direct des-
cendant of the black sheep Deveril even existed—or that James
Allingham and his own powerful yearnings would disrupt her
plan entirely.

Penny Jordan's first Harlequin Signature Edition *Love's Choices* was an
outstanding success. Penny Jordan has written more than 40 best-sell-
ing titles—more than 4 million copies sold.

Now, be sure to buy her latest bestseller, *Stronger Than Yearning*. Available wherever paperbacks are sold—in October.

Six exciting series for you every month... from Harlequin

Harlequin Romance·
The series that started it all

Tender, captivating and heartwarming...
love stories that sweep you off to faraway places
and delight you with the magic of love.

◆

Harlequin Presents·

Powerful contemporary love
stories...as individual as the
women who read them

The No. 1 romance series...
exciting love stories for you, the woman of today...
a rare blend of passion and dramatic realism.

◆

Harlequin Superromance®

It's more than romance...
it's Harlequin Superromance

A sophisticated, contemporary romance-fiction
series, providing you with a longer,
more involving read...a richer mix of complex plots,
realism and adventure.

Harlequin
American Romance™
Harlequin celebrates the
American woman...

...by offering you romance stories written
about American women, by American women
for American women. This series offers you
contemporary romances uniquely North American
in flavor and appeal.

◆

Harlequin Temptation
Passionate stories for
today's woman

An exciting series of sensual, mature stories of
love...dilemmas, choices, resolutions...
all contemporary issues dealt with in a true-to-life
fashion by some of your favorite authors.

◆

Harlequin Intrigue
Because romance can be quite
an adventure

Harlequin Intrigue, an innovative series that
blends the romance you expect...
with the unexpected. Each story has an added
element of intrigue that provides a new twist to
the Harlequin tradition of romance excellence.

Harlequin Books·